❀❀ ❀❀ ❀❀

"LEAVE HER ALONE." IT WAS DAVID Beckett, loud and bossy, coming to my defense. As if I needed him.

That was what did it.

I stood up.

"What's wrong, Claudia?"

I glimpsed Vivian's frown. Then her mouth slowly shaped an "o," everything moving in slow motion, my own hands feeling thick and strange as I unbuttoned my shirt, pulled it off and stood there feeling the hot sun on my flesh.

Another Fawcett Juniper Book
by Sonia Levitin:

THE YEAR OF SWEET SENIOR INSANITY

SMILE LIKE A PLASTIC DAISY

Sonia Levitin

FAWCETT JUNIPER • NEW YORK

The author gives special thanks to
Carol Agate, attorney,
and Rosemary M. Claire, educator,
for their generous help
and stimulating discussions.

RLI: $\dfrac{\text{VL: grades } 5 + \text{up}}{\text{IL: grades } 7 + \text{up}}$

A Fawcett Juniper Book
Published by Ballantine Books
Copyright © 1984 by Sonia Levitin

Library of Congress Catalog Card Number: 83-15616

ISBN 0-449-70120-4

This edition published by arrangement with Atheneum

Manufactured in the United States of America

First Ballantine Books Edition: July 1986

For Lloyd,
whose love and
understanding light my way . . .
and in memory of Annemarie Ewing Towner,
loving friend, teacher,
poet.

The token woman arrives like a milkbottle on the stoop
coming full and departing emptied.

The token woman carries a bouquet of hothouse celery
and a stenographer's pad; she will take
the minutes, perk the coffee, smile
like a plastic daisy and put out
the black cat of her sensuous anger
to howl on the fence all night.

—*from* "The Token Woman"
by Marge Piercy

from *Living in the Open*, copyright © 1976 by Marge Piercy, published by Alfred A. Knopf.

1

My name is Claudia Warner. Maybe you've heard about me. But wait, before you jump to conclusions. Just because my name was in the newspapers and everything doesn't mean I go around looking for trouble.

The thing is, I'm not one to make waves. Usually people don't even remember me. I'm not a soch or a rah-rah; I just play flute in the band. I take journalism and a light schedule for senior year. I'm not trying to win any medals or offices. My only goal was to get into Durant College, but that went down the tubes even before this mess. Durant College wants "students of distinction." This doesn't include me.

What I'm trying to explain is that I was as shocked as anyone else by what I did at that swim meet just about a month ago.

When my friend Bennie Murphy (her real name's Benicia) heard about it, she burst into tears. That's Bennie. Sweet and almost too sensitive. Her parents completely run her life.

Vivian, of course, was there. Maybe she didn't understand, but she never criticized, either. That's another pretty fabulous friend.

When it was over, and I sat in the vice-principal's office shaking, my teeth chattering, I began to think about all the people I knew and what they'd say. Surely Pete would hear about it. He goes to U.C. Santa Barbara, about one hundred miles north of here, but those kids have a regular grapevine to Menominee.

Menominee is my town, a jumbled-up place with its own school district, town council and courthouse. Menominee used to be country; a dairy, a stable and some small farms are still left. Mostly it's fairly new tract houses, some beautiful hillside homes and the town pride, our new shopping mall and civic center.

People here usually mind their own business—until there's a scandal. Then—look out. Even the kids away at college get the news. I was sure Pete would hear about it in a matter of hours. Then what?

I'd never gone with anyone before Pete. Oh, in middle school, but that's different; it doesn't really mean anything. In my junior year Pete and I became a couple. It changed me. I felt older, more serious—you know, *settled*.

It was comfortable with Pete. We talked a lot, and we laughed at silly things. Every night he'd phone and tell me what he'd done that day. Funny, how he'd tell me every little thing, like what brand of tennis shoes he was buying and how long he had to wait in line at the post office. My mother said Pete would make some girl a good husband. After he got an education, of course. She couldn't go to college herself, so she's big on education.

Pete had said he loved me—oh, yes, he told me every day last summer. We'd go down to our special little cove at the beach. It's private there, a litle place surrounded by rocks, and two or three cypresses growing close together, like a secret room. We'd talk and dream, and we would kiss, and gently he'd touch my breasts and murmur, "I love you, Claudia, I love you. I'll miss you so when I'm away."

I saw Pete over Christmas vacation, and once he asked

me to come up to Santa Barbara for a fraternity party. Otherwise we were in a sort of holding pattern. We'd agreed to go out with other people. Somehow, I didn't feel like being with any of the guys I knew. All the exciting boys were taken. It was discouraging.

Occasionally Pete phoned me. Like he was just checking to see whether we were still "together." After what happened at the swim meet, I had this terrible feeling about what would happen between us. I dreaded it; he'd be furious. Hurt. Another part of me countered: but why should he be? Does he think he owns me? No, no—but we love each other. We really do. I mean, we've been going together for a long time, so maybe I owe him something. You can't imagine the turmoil. A hundred times I argued it within myself. Still, I couldn't be sure how Pete would react.

I knew exactly what my mother would say. *How could you?*

Her face was frozen between disbelief and horror. "How *could* you?"

I looked up, not meeting her eyes, but past her. It was the only way to handle it, shrugging it off. Trying not to care, while inside I felt as if I'd eaten something spoiled and was about to vomit it up.

"It's not such a big deal," I said.

"Not a big deal?"

"If it was," I said, "they'd have called you sooner. It happened Tuesday. This is Thursday." Again I shrugged.

"You kept this from me for *three days!*"

Mom's eyes were like pale blue disks. She always looks faintly surprised because of the arch of her brows. Now it was like a game, she trying not to show her distress, I trying to pretend it didn't matter. I wondered vaguely when we had started playing these games. Maybe on the day I was born.

I repeated, "It's no big deal. Dr. Wallenburg wouldn't have made such a federal case out of it. It's all because she

3

was gone and old Milden took over. Cave Milden. How could you expect anyone to be normal with a first name like *Cave?"*

My voice held an edge of hysteria. Mom was biting her lip.

"Claudia, I'm trying to understand. I get a letter from the principal's office. You are suspended from school. I hear there's near rioting at the school for two days in a row. Now Mr. Milden says that if you continue this defiance . . ."

"I did not defy him. The fact is, they were wrong to suspend me."

My mother stared. "I can't believe this, Claudia. It's beyond me."

I clenched my teeth to keep from screaming. So much is beyond her, that's the trouble. Bicycling, swimming in the ocean, eating pizza—all that was beyond her! She might as well be living in the eighteenth century. I stood appraising her and she me, and I guess we were both baffled at how we can be so different yet look so alike. My hair isn't uniformly blonde like hers, but then, she has help. Our mouths, people say, are identical, and also our stature. We stood at eye level.

"I simply don't understand you, Claudia. I don't know what I'll tell your father."

"Maybe you won't have to tell him anything."

"This letter has to be signed by your parents."

"Pretend I just have one parent."

"You're stuck with two," she said, sarcastic.

"Do you have to show him the letter?"

"You know I do."

"Why?"

Her hands flew up for a moment, fluttered down to her sides. "It's obvious," she said. "He would expect me to tell him."

"And you always do what he expects."

Mom's features tensed. "Don't turn this around," she

4

snapped. "We were talking about you! What you did at the swim meet on Tuesday."

"Not only me. Another girl, Marsha McClure and a couple of freshmen, did it too. We all did it."

"But you were the ring leader."

"Oh, *Mom*."

"Why did you do it?" Mom's eyes glittered. "To make a statement?"

"Yeah. A statement. You wouldn't understand."

"You're right." Now anger stood in her eyes, spread in a blush over her cheeks. "I always had to behave myself like a lady. My parents were dirt poor, but we had standards. Self-control. Decency. Whatever happened to those?"

"Maybe your generation killed all that in Vietnam!" I screamed.

"Oh, come on, Claudia!" She turned on me, furious, her hand raised. "How can you blame your obnoxious behavior on my generation? It's got nothing to do with Vietnam or anything like it."

"It's got everything to do with it! Everything!" My heart pounded. Visions and words leaped before my eyes—Mr. Xavier's words, so brilliant and undeniably true that after one of his lectures every student in the class had risen simultaneously and applauded.

"Nothing happens in a vacuum," I cried, panting and breathless. "Everything in society is interrelated. You can't go around killing innocent women and children, digging pits and shooting them in jungle outposts, and then talk to your children about obscenity and manners and—"

"I need to go to the market," said my mother. "You're crazy. We're out of milk."

"I don't want milk! I hate milk!"

The door slammed violently; the windows rattled.

Well, you won't be able to understand unless you know the whole story from the beginning. Things hinge on each

5

other; who can ever say, *this* is the cause, or *that* is how it happened. To understand what I did at the swim meet, you have to go back at least to the beginning of senior year and know the kind of person I was. Because—understand this!—since then, I have changed.

2

Senior year, Claudia and Vivian had decided they'd just coast, enjoy senior activities, take the SAT's, no hard electives. Bennie was taking senior math and chemistry and walking around like a zombie with stacks of books under her arms. Well, she had what Dr. Wallenburg called "definite goals." To Vivian and Claudia, senior year was a time for trading memories, getting close to the people and things they'd soon leave behind—a time to be mellow.

Then came Mr. Xavier. He caught Claudia like a tidal wave or a landslide. She was totally unprepared.

It happened that at spring break, Claudia's senior problems class split into two electives, economics or government. She chose the latter.

"Economics is tough going, Claudia," her dad had warned. "Especially if you're not strong in math. I had to fight to get through that course in college."

So Claudia signed up for government with Mr. Xavier. She'd heard rumors about him—the kids in his classes were like a cult. All they did was roll their eyes and groan with mysterious delight and say he was absolutely fantastic, fantastic, but they didn't explain. That first day in class,

Claudia got it. It hit her with such force that she felt numb afterward and tongue-tied, stumbling out into the glaring sun, dazed.

She had gone to the lunch pavillion, cutting band rehearsal, high on the echo of his voice, the intensity of his expressions, his words. His first name was Philip. She sat there thinking it—Philip, remembering:

"I am Philip Xavier. I am here not to teach you, because nobody can teach anybody anything—it must all come from within. The word 'education' stems from *educar,* to lead, and all I can profess to do is to lead you to some hypotheses, help you open a few doors. Most people don't want you to open those doors. Oh, we talk a lot about freedom, but at the same time most of the information you receive is carefully channeled, censored or, at the very least, denied to you by social pressure.

"Now, I never give pop quizzes. That's a stupid game, a waste of your time and mine. I will give you a three-hour final, an open book test, and you can bring in whatever sources you like.

"This text, which our school district has in its wisdom seen fit to distribute, is boring, repetitive and filled with half-truths. I'm handing it out because it's a state require-ment. If you're a masochist, you can read it. Otherwise, just use it for a doorstop. Now, let's talk about government. Let's find out who really runs things in this country. At the beginning there were a few rich men who owned many slaves and lots of land, and they decided to preserve this bounty for themselves, so they wrote the . . ."

At the end of it, Claudia had emerged stunned. Philip Xavier was a new force in her life. Everything changed. She thought about him constantly.

Gone were her notions of lazy days, of indifference to her clothes, of inattention to the changing times outside the small cocoon of Menominee. Mr. Xavier made demands, not overtly, but by who he was and by her need for his notice.

8

Claudia sat in the very middle of the room, keen to his every gesture and expression. She stayed after class to gather his afterthoughts like a starving pup licking the last scraps. She wrote down every reference and rushed to the library to get the books, ready for discussion, rewarded by his smile. He loved a good controversy; it brought a flush to his face and ardor into his voice. Once he said, when everyone else had left, "That was an ingenious argument you made today, Claudia." (She had read it the past night in Plato's *Republic*.) And then, inexplicably, he touched her arm and said softly, "It takes courage to be happy, my dear."

Her throat had tightened with joy. *My dear*.

He had a free sixth period. So did Claudia. She tried not to resent the other students who also came to his room. Soon they formed a small group of devotees, often wandering outdoors to sit on the lawn under a shade tree. Mr. Xavier would sit cross-legged, plucking out bits of grass as he listened, flexing his fingers when he spoke: Claudia could hardly bear to look at him, did not know where to fix her eyes.

Vivian knew. "You have really got it bad."

"Don't be silly. He's just very brilliant. And exciting."

"Sure."

It all had a strange, dreamy quality, as though time and the grass and sky met here where Mr. Xavier sat, his back pressed against the rough bark of the maple tree, the gleam in his eyes mirroring the flash of sunlight on the leaves as they twirled and danced when the breeze came. Yet the *now* was wrapped into the past, with all its fantasies and its sorrows, because of David Beckett.

He, too, was in Mr. Xavier's class. It was the first class they ever had together; and after all these years it seemed that David Beckett had grown just so he could sit in the same circle with Mr. Xavier, so that she would have to watch. The two men were much alike, but so different! It

9

taunted and tormented her, their similarities, their differences. David, too, knew how to use words, how to draw everybody's attention, how to create that turmoil in her.

David Beckett totally ignored her.

Why? And why, after all this time, did she still care?

She hated herself for caring, carrying a crush since the age of thirteen—what an idiot! What a *child!* Still, she could not break herself of that plunging feeling in her chest whenever he walked by, the swift perking of interest when his name came up, or the ritual she had developed. In the night, just before she fell asleep, she summoned his voice and his face. And she thought of what they might do together, how it might feel, and then she thought of how he would gaze at her with those eyes of teal blue.

Nobody else had eyes like that; they had astonished her from the start, when she was in seventh grade and they met at their lockers and started to talk.

From then on they walked home together every afternoon and spoke on the phone every night, once until two in the morning, whispering. The next day when they walked to school, they held hands all the way, and behind a hedge he first kissed her.

David played tennis and was entered in the regional competition. He had won a bronze medal. Claudia went on Saturdays to watch him play, astounded by that look on his face when he plunged into competition—tense, fiery, superbly controlled.

That February the accident happened. Suddenly his name became public property. David Beckett, the victim, hit by a van while riding a dirt bike on Walnut Boulevard. He was thrown twenty feet into the air.

After months in the hospital his jaw worked properly, and he could walk again. He would never again play tennis. Of course, he was lucky to be alive, though he had missed so much school, they had to put him back a year.

Back at school, the teal blue eyes glinted even more

sharply. During his confinement, Claudia had telephoned him four different times. He was brief and sullen.

The day he finally returned to school, Claudia hid from him, looked for him, finally found the courage to appear in his path. Her mouth was dry, her lips wavering over the syllables. "David—hi! Are you feeling all right?"

He answered, "Sure. First rate."

It was language he had never used before; it signified the change in him. She wanted to ask why he hadn't let her come to visit, but he turned away.

"David, I missed you." It took all her courage to say it.

He turned once more, and she saw a wildness in his eyes, almost bordering on cruelty, and he said, "Sorry for the inconvenience." It was the last time they spoke.

His new friends, Julian Margolis and Bob Greene, were brash and big. All three were in Claudia's government class. All seemed to know exactly what the world held in store for them—it was like a large fruit out of which they would eat the pulp and suck the juice.

That was the unbearable thing, their assurance, while Claudia and her friends sat and sighed, growing tired, still unenlightened. What to do? Where to begin? Who could tell them?

Vivian was going to Berkeley. Claudia had also been accepted to the U.C. system and could choose between Berkeley and Santa Barbara. Durant College up north had sent her a rejection letter early in March. She hadn't realized until then how much she'd wanted to go to Durant, for the prestige as much as for its methods.

Bennie's parents had enrolled her at Pomona College years ago. She talked of studying microbiology.

Vivian and Claudia challenged her. "Why do you want to do that?"

"I like to know what makes things tick."

"Then be a watchmaker!" Vivian and Claudia laughed, and Bennie sweetly smiled and shook her head at their silliness.

"I know what I'm going to do," Vivian declared. She had known for three years. "After two years of college I'll go work for the airlines."

Bennie marveled. "Will your parents let you?"

"Pooh. It's my life."

"Maybe I'll be a vet," Claudia said, testing it.

"What kind?" asked Bennie, interested.

"Elephant." Claudia giggled. "When I travel to see my patients I won't need to bring a trunk."

They fell over themselves laughing. "Oh, my God," they chorused, "you're crazy. You're absolutely too much."

She wanted to be a little crazy, doing hilarious things, like Fay Allison and Joanie Truitt, that wildly spontaneous pair. They did incredible, exciting things. If she were just a little crazy and more spontaneous, her eyebrows would straighten out. Smiling does that—stretches the face, especially the brows. Maybe she'd get the glow that shone from girls like Sissy Goldstein and Denise Hunt, who won elections and awards. Actually, she didn't want to be like those gushing, shrieking girls. She just wanted to be— what?

She never knew what to answer when her parents' friends came over and inquired, as if they really cared, "What are your plans, Claudia?"

She would mumble and stammer and try to smile, until her father would finally speak up. "She's considering teaching. Aren't you, honey."

"Yes."

"Maybe she'll go into business. Lots of opportunity for women in business these days. Maybe I could get her a place with one of my accounts. You know, I do all the insurance for the Westfield chain. Or she might help Scott and me."

Scott, her brother, was studying business administration. He planned to go into their father's business. The two of them were already developing a special language, separating them further from "the girls."

Once her mother had asked her, "What do you really want, Claudia?"

"I guess—" Claudia had hesitated, looking outside to the street, as if there she might find answers. "I guess—to be like you. Get married and have kids, and a little job that's fun. You know. To bring in some of my own money. I don't know."

Her mother's eyes had glistened, and she smiled, came alive, her hands and her words tumbling, rushing. "Oh, yes, that's right. I'm a very lucky woman to have you and Scott and to be married to a man who is . . . who doesn't mind . . . well, you know. And I love my job. It's really very creative. I get to meet so many interesting people."

For three years now, since Scott left for college, her mom had been selling LovLee Cosmetics. She sold them, like Tupperware, to groups of women at parties. Sometimes she made special house calls to just one or two women.

"It's given me a whole new lease on life," she would tell her friends. "It's so stimulating. Really."

That night Claudia had lain in her bed unable to sleep. LovLee Cosmetics in their perfect pink boxes with the white embossed hearts stood on her bureau. The smell of them was suffocating.

She got up, shoved the boxes into her bottom bureau drawer and lay down again, breathing heavily, thinking with each breath, *I'd rather die than sell LovLee Cosmetics* . . .

It wasn't until months later, in Mr. Xavier's class, that Claudia discovered exactly what she wanted to do and also whom she wanted to be like in every way.

Glenda French.

3

"Who's Glenda French?"

Vivian was the first to hear about her.

"She's absolutely fabulous. A lawyer. Mr. Xavier had her come to talk to our class. She told us about civil rights. Protest marches in the fifties. Did you know black people couldn't even vote? Couldn't even ride the same buses . . . ?"

"Yeah. I know a bunch of people went down there to help. Did she go there? To Mississippi?"

"No, no. She was just a baby then. She's twenty-eight now."

"Xavier's girlfriend?"

"Of course not!" Impatiently Claudia stamped her foot. "She's a fabulous lawyer! She knows everything. About the student sit-ins of the sixties. Now she's working for ERA. Listen, the things she told us . . ."

Vivian stared, smiled, nodded, and once or twice she said, "Wow."

Claudia wished she could make Vivian understand. "She's like a super-star. Like Mick Jagger or—or Linda Ronstadt!"

Vivian stared, holding back laughter. "Oh, God, Claudia, I love you!"

Claudia's heart pounded; she was almost frightened. "Something is happening to me," she confessed, breathless. "I want to be . . ." She sighed. ". . . different. If you'd seen Glenda. She's so wonderful. She told us things . . ."

But it was impossible to duplicate Glenda's passion or gestures or intensity. "Never in the history of the world, my friends, has any group ever won a right without a struggle! A bloody struggle! Never!"

Workers battling in the street; the Haymarket riots in Chicago where strikers were clubbed and beaten; little children working in factories, twelve, fourteen hours a day, until they fell asleep over their machines and were dumped out onto the streets—how could one believe it? How could one *not* believe—the soul said it was true. It had really happened.

"I'm not inventing stories to amaze or distress you." Glenda's eyes held a catlike ferocity, a rage inspired by the truth. "This is all documented. We sit here in our little cocoons, and we feel safe. And smug. Oh, it happened long ago, we say. Nothing like it can happen again." She paused, stared at them with her large, exquisite eyes. "Don't you believe it. Don't let yourselves be blinded!"

"She was fabulous," Claudia told her parents that night. "Beautiful and smart. She knows everything about the law. She told us how in the sixties in Berkeley some kids were trying to plant vegetables in a park, and the police came with tear gas and riot sticks . . ."

Claudia felt charged and exhilarated. The drumming inside led her on with a bursting need to tell it! Tell it! She would hold her parents captive and astounded as Glenda had held her. That feeling of power brought the right words to her lips and that gleam into her eyes—she could feel it.

"Yeah, I remember that," said her father. "I was just out

of college myself. They were nothing but a bunch of hippies strung out on dope."

Claudia gasped. "They brought in helicopters, Dad, and police with tear gas. Those were students. They were just expressing their opinions. Glenda says that under the first amendment of the Constitution—"

"Who is this Glenda? Somebody taking around petitions?"

"Don't you ever listen to me? I just told you. She's a woman Mr. Xavier had in class today. A lawyer. *Daddy!*"

Easy, she told herself. Speak slowly, distinctly, the way Glenda French spoke, with her eyes snapping and jaw firm.

"For the first time, ever," Claudia said, "I can see what's happening. How everything is related. History is real. Things that happen in government are—are predictable. Nothing just happens by coincidence. Did you know that the FBI was giving LSD to people in the sixties? Did you know that our own state department was testing—?"

"Listen, baby, you're all worked up. Doreen, isn't there something else to eat? I've had three helpings of salad."

Claudia's mother rose quickly. "Sure. Just a minute. It's all ready."

"The thing is, Daddy, people just go around assuming that whatever the government does is all right. But it isn't always. After all, our government at the beginning actually sanctioned slavery. The Constitution was written by—"

"Claudia, would you mind getting me a glass of water?"

"I forgot the water, Walt," said her mother.

Claudia got the water. Her hand shook slightly as she set down the glass.

Her mother served the roasted chicken on a platter. Her father speared a piece of chicken, looked at it appraisingly, then let it fall to his plate.

"So," he said, cutting off a large piece. "I suppose now you want to be a lawyer." He chewed quickly, briskly.

16

Claudia stared at him. She nodded. "I've been thinking about it."

He nodded, chewing. "Think you can get through three years of law school? After college?"

"Lawyers make a lot of money," said her mother.

"I suppose I could," Claudia said. "I mean, if you really want something bad enough—I know it's hard. But . . ."

"Anything worthwhile is hard," her father said. "Remember what I always said? When you were little?"

Claudia nodded, feeling flushed and miserable. "Stick," she mumbled.

"Be a postage stamp!" her father said, beaming. "Stick until the job's done! This woman lawyer. I guess she's one of those militants."

Claudia sighed. "I don't know."

"Wants to change the world." He smiled wryly.

Claudia's mother smiled too, the way she did when Dad came around with his Polaroid camera. He liked to catch them unawares. "Smile!"

He had finished his chicken and pushed his plate away. "Well, honey, if you want to be a lawyer, if you're really serious and will work hard—we'll see. You know I'll pay for your education. Same as Scott's. Meanwhile . . ." He tossed his napkin lightly onto his dish. ". . . if you want to change the world, I have a suggestion for you."

Claudia felt a strange churning in her chest, not from his words, but from something in his tone.

Her mother spoke tensely. "What is it, Walt?"

"She wants to change the world, she should start by cleaning her room. That place is a pigpen. The cat's been sleeping in there, I can tell."

Furious, Claudia rose, scraped her chair away from the table.

"What's the matter with her? I said she could go to law school, didn't I?" He blew out a huff of air. "Last month she wanted to be a vet."

17

"It's the age, Walt . . ."

In her bedroom Claudia reached for Chaucer, the cat, the black monster-darling with golden eyes, silky fur and high curling tail. The cat had been a concession to Claudia when Scott went away to college. The battle of the cat in the bedroom had raged from the start. Almost as if her father enjoyed it.

Involuntarily, Claudia shuddered. The cat leaped away, leaving a long scratch on her arm. For a moment Claudia relished the pain, the faint line of blood. Pain was better than the shuddering emptiness she felt, better than the contempt and hatred that made her never want to tell her father anything again. How many times had she opened herself up, only to be humiliated by a pat, a joke, a laugh. Well, never again. She would share nothing. Better yet, feel nothing.

For the first time it seemed that a choice stood clear before her. She could choose from two kinds of becoming— force herself into that pose of cool aloofness, never expressing a strong opinion, never open to distress. Then she would not annoy people. She could remain among the many empty, silent ones. Or she could be counted. Like Glenda.

After class Claudia had gone up to see her. Up close, she was even more vibrant; her smile was like something electric in the air, and Claudia felt stunned by it, warmed. "I wanted to talk to you," she said, feeling her own smile bursting, glowing. "I'd love to be a lawyer! Like you. Is it hard?"

Glenda laughed. A wonderful, beautiful laugh. "Not hard going. What's hard is deciding, realizing you can be anything you really want to be. That was the struggle I had to overcome. At one time I never thought I'd even graduate high school."

"How could that be?" Claudia had asked, astonished.

"It's a long story." Smiling, she touched Claudia's arm.

"Maybe Mr. Xavier will let me come back again. We could talk about that whole sexist thing."

Mr. Xavier heard her. "Anytime, Glenda," he said. Then, "Why don't you list some books for these girls to read. We haven't gone into any of the feminist literature."

Glenda became serious. She gazed at Claudia, her dark eyes like magnets, drawing her close. "You haven't read any? Then, try these." She scribbled down titles, rapidly. "And these. And this one. You haven't read *any?* What's your name? Claudia. Read these. Then we'll talk."

A challenge. A promise.

Claudia had gone to the library on her bike right after school. Usually she drove, but her mother's car was "acting up again." It was a good excuse to take an eight-mile bike ride, like a kid again. She loved to ride fast, pumping and pumping, imagining herself speeding down a runway in preparation for flight. What must it be like to ride a motorcycle? To open it up, full speed, to leap over the bumps and land, roar off again—of course, she never would. Those things were dangerous. Her parents would kill her.

Her parents didn't like speed. They didn't like noise. They didn't like excitement.

"Slow down!" her father's favorite admonition. "It isn't wise," her mother's usual comment. All her mom had ever done was to play Ping-Pong. "I won first place at summer camp when I was just about your age!"

It baffled Claudia, how anyone could let that last for a life-time. Her mother didn't like sweat or heat or smells. "Your hands smell funny," she'd say, backing off.

Home from the library, sweaty and exulting, Claudia had piled all the books on her desk, planning to spend tonight reading. But now she had no will to open them. The anger at her father left her despondent, drained.

She wrote out her Spanish homework, going through the motions with only half a mind. Not a sound came from the

19

living room. Her father would be reading some dull insurance journals. Once in a while he allowed himself a paperback detective novel.

Her mother would be sitting at the little wicker desk, going over her receipts. She kept all her papers in a twelve-pocket file that Dad had brought her from the office. He presented it with a grand flourish. "For my working girl," he said, beaming. He was proud of Mom's job. He told people about it, looking pleased. "It's a good idea for a woman to have something extra to occupy her mind. After all, when the kids get older . . ."

For Claudia, getting older had seemed to be an uneven, exhausting process that always caught her by surprise. She remembered preschool, dancing round and round with a lovely multicolored scarf trailing over her shoulders. She remembered brushing the hamster with an old toothbrush and making finger paintings in red and blue. And suddenly she was in fourth grade, loving her teacher, loving the penmanship lessons everyone else hated, hearing a flute solo for the first time, memorizing the poem called "Trees." Next came that awful summer of being twelve-almost-thirteen, when everything changed.

People became horrible to her. Clerks in stores eyed her with amusement and whispered about her, for everything she wore looked wrong. Her hair was dull. Her face was blotched. No wonder even her own brother couldn't stand to be near her. They had once wrestled on the lawn. They had once tumbled together in the ocean and built elaborate sand-people to lie like friendly giants on the shore. That all ended the summer she was twelve-almost-thirteen.

That summer it seemed she spent the entire time sitting on the old hammock at the far end of the yard. The hammock stood under the olive tree, and she could smell the dry bark and hear the brittle leaves and the hard, bitter fruit dropping down onto the ground. Olives were poisonous, someone had told her, until they were properly ripened and marinated. We are growing poison in our yard, she thought morosely, turning the idea over and over in her mind, pondering it the way she also pondered the huge spider's web, complete with its ghastly host, strung between the tree and the fence. One day she saw a fallen bird's egg smashed on the ground, and she cried.

She cried a lot that summer. She had no friends. One had left for Chicago. Another moved away. The third went to camp, and the fourth had never really been her friend anyway. The only thing that saved her was the flute. She played for hours.

By the end of that summer Claudia felt strangely exhausted. Her mother gazed at her with worry, wondering aloud whether she was getting enough rest. She cooked plenty of crisp vegetables, kept a supply of apples and cookies on hand. It did no good. Claudia still grew and cried and wore hollows beneath her eyes where the skin seemed too transparent, giving away her secret.

She dreaded the first day of junior high and P.E. She had heard about the shared dressing rooms and communal showers. She thought she'd die.

In midsummer her mother had begun talking about it. "We'll have to go and buy you some bras."

Claudia found ways to be busy, to be absent, to catch a cold or to insist upon her pure hatred for that particular department store.

Her mother looked puzzled. Another shop, then? Perhaps one of those nice little shops in the mall? Really, dear, it's getting to be ridiculous.

Claudia had burst into tears.

Finally, in August, her mother caught her one day. From the supermarket she drove directly to the department store.

The lingerie section was enormous, with a million varieties of undergarments to choose from. Obviously, there were people who didn't mind selecting and discussing these things.

The saleslady and her mother seemed to have a conspiracy going; they smiled at each other in a twinkling way.

"My daughter wants to buy some bras."

"Ah, yes. Let me show you what we have."

Smiles, twinkling eyes, fleet fingers rippling through layers of soft fabric. "Would she like something soft? Plunging? White or nude or maybe pink? Some of the young girls like these bright colors. Lots of them are buying these little body huggers, as they're called—what size cup?"

Cup. My cup runneth over. Oh, God.

"I believe that would be too small."

"Do you think a B then? Or even a . . . ? Here, we'll try several. You can never tell until you try them on."

In the dressing room the sales lady was happy. "My, that's nice bust development. She'll need some good support."

Claudia wanted to die.

Her mother urged Claudia to buy four bras. Claudia, gritting her teeth, wanted to buy one. They compromised. Two. Her mother gave the saleslady a look. "We'll be back," she murmured faintly.

If her father noticed, he graciously said nothing. But when he approached her later that night for some inconsequential reason, she involuntarily flung up her arms, and in the next instant hated herself for it. And she hated him for making her feel so—so *conspicuous.*

One day she heard him saying, "She's getting to be a big kid, Doreen. Bigger than you ever were."

"Hush now, Walt. You know how sensitive young girls are."

Her mother's friends, over for coffee in the afternoon, took curious delight in Claudia's bosom. "Lovely girl. Well developed. Pretty soon the boys will be lining up for her."

"I won't let her date yet."

"Well, I mean . . ."

And once she heard Scott cuss at his friend and yell, "I'll smash your face in! You just lay off my sister!"

When she walked on the street, truck drivers began to scream out at her. "Whoo—oo! Girlie!" She used to rollerskate on the sidewalk, cruising down like a demon, hair flying. But then—guys on motorbikes started to turn their heads as they zoomed past, and they hollered out from the roar of their machines, "Hey, baby! Wanna . . . ?"

The last word was always lost in the wind. Was it? Or did her mind refuse to acknowledge and translate what her new body meant to them?

4

Her father had left early, as he did every third Saturday.

"Walt's fishing day," her mother explained to friends. "It's good for him to get off on his own. It eases the pressure."

As though her father lived inside a huge, boiling pot that threatened to explode. Pieces of flesh and bone might fly across the room, sticking to the ceiling, as had happened years ago when Mom cooked a chicken in the old pressure cooker and something went wrong.

On Saturday mornings Mom cleaned. After breakfast Claudia stood watching her for a few moments. She hummed as she scrubbed the grout between the kitchen tiles.

"Guess I'll go clean my room," Claudia said.

Her mother smiled approvingly. "Good girl. Later will you come with me to take the car in? I hate going alone to that part of—"

"Sure. I'll take care of you."

"Sass-pot!" she said, but smiling.

Claudia cleaned her room. Then she took her feminist books out to the hammock. Chaucer followed. He scam-

24

pered up a stout limb of the olive tree and there puffed up, tail hanging down.

Claudia began to read. And she slipped away into thoughts that were oddly familiar. Old refrains sang in her mind, melancholy songs to make her weep. Why so blue, Claudia? She's in another mood, don't you know? Girls are so emotional. My, baby, you're cute when you're mad.

Too familiar, the words and the thoughts; she felt strangled by them, yet released from some safe haven all at once, too fast. Yes, she could see it now. That writhing uneasiness inside her, felt for years! buried for years! it had a reason. They called her silly, hysterical, stubborn, moody. They had made her feel like an alien on this planet, or a witch; something radically wrong with her, always sullen and silently enraged. They made her feel misfit and misshapen, and so in her dreams and in dark moments she plotted her child's revenge. She had to get even. But how? She had to show them. But what? That being a girl held no shame! No inferiority. That being a girl was OK.

Claudia lay with the book open upon her chest. All the women she had read about were her kin. And she knew their pain:

The Chinese girls whose poor feet were bound and mutilated.

Moslem girls, circumsized to prevent sexual pleasure, to keep them at home.

Little babies born female, cast outside the city wall to die of exposure or be eaten by wolves.

The women—oh, the thousands—shamed for being "possessed" during their menstrual flow, called unclean, accused of poisoning the wells during their monthly curse.

And the good Christian fathers who beat their wives for speaking in church or at market . . . and the lords who claimed the peasants' daughters for their lust . . . and the masters who whipped their black slave girls, then used them to make more slaves. . . .

Claudia lay on the hammock, aching, exhausted. She who had never had a sister, now had sisters, thousands and millions of them united by pain or, if not pain, then mere drudgery. Rising at dawn to wash the clothes and tend the babies; pregnant again and without shoes. It was the pioneer women who drew icy water from the well, brought it up to the house in buckets, set it to boiling before the men came in wanting breakfast. Nameless, they died in the wilderness. Their husbands, settled, sent for new wives from the east.

Claudia picked up the book. It had been written by a professor, a man. More than anything at this moment, she wished to see this man, to look into his eyes, to tell him, yes, it is true. She had always known, deep down, what the world really thought of women. Her mother had taught her that. Oh, it was a subtle training. *Speak softly, dear, don't be so wild. Let your brother do that. Honey, you mustn't sit that way.*

Little girls are loved for their weakness. They are taught to smile when they meet people, to wash well and hide their smells. Girls are expected to cry, are given hugs and kisses when they cry, because everyone knows their tears are swiftly triggered—and since they can't do figures or think logically, teach 'em to play a nice instrument, nothing too loud.

From the house Claudia heard her mother singing an old song. "You are always in my heart . . . !"

She closed her eyes, turned her head against the rough fabric of the hammock. She could smell the dust and leaf mold of many seasons. She could remain here, private and safe. She could let it all go, continue being the same Claudia Warner, a nice girl who played flute, had a few friends, didn't ever make waves.

But Claudia picked up the book again. It fell open. Incredibly, and for the first time in her life, she saw her own name printed on a page.

"In Roman times," it said, "girls were so little regarded that they did not even have their own names. Thus the daughter of Claudius became Claudia. Her sisters might all bear the same name, being called Claudia the Second, Third, etc., or Claudia the Younger."

Claudia stared at the page. Then she let out a shriek so sudden that Chaucer leapt from the branch and fled into the thickets as Claudia ran to the house shouting, "Mother! *Mother!*"

Her mother, talking on the telephone, had been annoyed at the interruption. Later, from her room, Claudia heard her talking to her friend in that certain low voice that suggested they were discussing her. She only heard one word: "Impossible."

Afterward, Mom came into her room, smiling for a fresh start. Claudia smiled back.

"Ready to go to the garage with me?"

"Sure. How will we get back?"

"If they need to keep the car we'll take a cab."

Her mother hated taking cabs alone. Claudia nodded. Maybe on the way over they could talk.

"Mom, did you ever wonder what you'd have done if you hadn't married Dad?"

They passed a tavern. Claudia stared at the banner. "FRIDAY NIGHT! WET T-SHIRT CONTEST! PRIZES!"

"Is there any beer left? Or did your dad take it fishing?"

"I don't know. *You* hate beer."

"He might want some for tomorrow. Maybe we should stop."

"You didn't answer my question."

"What question?" She made a left turn, concentrating.

"Forget it."

A minute or two later her mother replied. "I would have married someone else."

"How do you know?"

27

"Because I wanted to have children, for one thing. And because I like being married."

"How did you know you'd like it before you ever were?" Claudia reasoned.

"Oh, Claudia, you just know those things." She smiled. "Don't you want to get married?"

"I don't know."

"You don't know! What about Pete?"

"What about him?"

"I thought you two were in love."

"Yeah. Well. Actually, I don't know Pete all that well."

Her mother's lips kept the roundness of surprise for a long time. It was a comment she would repeat to her friends, puzzled, asking, "What do you make of that? Kids nowadays . . ."

She sighed and shook her head, so that her hair caught the sunlight. Her hair was very pretty. Everyone said so. "Actually," she said, "I have wondered about you and Pete."

"Don't worry, Mother. Pete and I never slept together."

Her mother kept her eyes straight ahead. Only a faintly perceptible stiffening of her nostrils showed her annoyance. "I didn't think you had."

"Why? Lots of girls do."

"Look, Claudia. Do we have to argue? I just wanted to tell you that if you—the thing is, you can talk to me. Or the doctor."

Claudia nodded, suddenly tearful. "Mom, I know that."

What she didn't know and couldn't bring herself to ask anyone was why the surging sweetness of her fantasies was nothing like the reality of Pete's kisses or his hands on her breasts. There had to be something terribly wrong with her.

"What I mean is," her mother continued, "when I was your age I had a lot of questions."

"And do you know all the answers now?" Claudia asked, sharp and sarcastic.

Her mother stiffened, kept silent until they pulled in at the garage. Then she arranged her face into a pleasant expression and called to an attendant. "Hi! I'm Mrs. Warner. Could I please talk to Randy? I called earlier and he said . . ."

In a moment a young fellow appeared, sauntering over with an easy, rolling gait, wiping his hands on a rag. He seemed too young to be a mechanic, but the badge on his pocket said "Randy."

He grinned, bent down with his elbow across Mom's window, his face close to her as he asked, "What can I do for you, sweetheart?"

Mom laughed, pulling back slightly. "I—I don't know. I think it might be the starter again. At least that's what my husband says. I don't know—would you mind checking it for me?"

"Sure." He prolonged his gaze, gave Claudia a quick wink and turned to delve under the hood, grunting, wiping his brow, at last bringing up a small part, running off to replace it, returning to explain what he had done.

"You see, dear, when this little groove wears down . . . only held by this pin . . . and when you slam on the brake . . ."

Mom listened, nodding, until he had finished. "Will it be all right now?" she asked.

"Good as new, sweetheart. And no charge for the labor. Just pay me for the part."

"Oh, that's wonderful."

"Say, do you want me to change your air filter while you're here?"

Mom frowned, bit her lip. "I don't know—does it need changing?"

"It's pretty dirty." He smiled, shook his head.

"I don't know—how much is it?"

"Only nine-fifty. It only takes a minute."

"I'm not sure when I last . . ."

"Well, why don't you check with your husband." He handed back her credit card, holding on for an extended moment, laughing.

"I'll do that," Mom said, smiling, shaking her head so that her hair waved and caught the light.

As they drove out, she looked in the rear view mirror, and Claudia knew she was looking at her face, not the traffic. Furious, she exploded, "Why do you let him call you sweetheart?"

"What?" Her mother whirled around, hitting the brake. "What are you talking about? That kid? He's just a kid!"

"Then why do you let him treat you as if you were a—a nitwit, or his *lover?*"

Her mother's face went white, then splotchy. Her voice was heavy. "Claudia, I've had just about enough. I resent your tone and the way you think you can say anything to me. I resent the implication that I have any interest in that—in a mechanic . . . !"

Claudia slipped down in the seat, turning her face toward the window. "Forget it," she mumbled.

"I think you owe me an apology."

"I'm sorry."

Her mother, gracious, not only allowed her to have the last word, but reached over and patted Claudia's hand.

Her parents, about to leave for the movies, stopped at the door. Her mother's gaze swept over her, reluctantly. "Want to come with us, Claudia?"

"What are you seeing?"

"What did we decide, Walt?"

"Oh, that spy movie. You know. Something about a needle. We'd better hurry. If you want to come, Claudia, get some shoes on."

Claudia stood rooted there, heavy with indecision. Should she go to the movie? She hated those spy stories. But she felt a terrible dread; it was a bad night to be alone.

"Well, are you coming or aren't you?" her father asked gruffly. "Make up your mind."

Tears threatened.

"Wait a minute, Walt," said her mother, taking a single step toward Claudia. Softly she asked, "Are you feeling all right?"

Claudia nodded. She tried a smile.

"Look, let's just forget the whole thing," said her father. "We'll stay home. I'd rather not go than come in late."

"No, no!" Claudia cried. "You two go ahead. I have some reading to do. Maybe Bennie or Viv will come over."

They left, and that feeling of dread once again engulfed her. She called Vivian. Vivian was already out with Yale. Bennie and her family were home, watching old movies. Claudia went to her room. It seemed preordained that she would confront those books again. There was no escape.

She read until she felt overloaded. She had to read. She had to see that over everything hangs the shadow of power, that fairness is a fiction, and law is twisted and coiled like a snake around a stick. And at the center of it, she had to see that elemental struggle. Woman. And man. From the beginning, in contest.

The cat lay staring up at her, tense and watchful.

She saw a new word. Misogyny. Hatred of women.

"Remember," wrote Abigail Adams, "all men would be tyrants if they could."

But, of course, her father let her mother spend all the money she wanted on her hair and her clothes. He loved her bright blondeness.

So did that mechanic, Randy. *Sweetheart. Dear. Dear, dumb blonde.*

She longed, suddenly, for Scott. If Scott were home they might talk. Or at least—and maybe better—she'd start a good, hot fight. One of them would end up with a nosebleed, some scratches. There'd be a lot of screaming

31

and slamming and racing back and forth, finally ending either in tears or that collapsing, hysterical laughter.

It had been years since they'd had one of those.

Last time she saw Scott, over Christmas, he had talked about his new girlfriend, Laura.

Mother asked, "Is she pretty?"

Dad had asked, "What's her major? Hope it's not philosophy or psychology. Or what's that new one? Recreational therapy?"

Scott replied, "She's thinking of architecture."

Dad let out a low whistle. "Good. She won't be bugging a guy about getting married."

Scott laughed, rubbed the back of his neck.

Mom asked, "Are you going steady?"

"Doreen," said their father, exasperated, "kids don't go steady these days. They have relationships. You're twenty years behind times."

Claudia returned to the books.

As she read, Chaucer watched. And there was nobody else to share the weight of her anger. It was like a sore or a sickness in her body, and nobody to help her heal.

5

Afterwards they all wanted to know: *Why* did you do it?
What could she tell them?

I don't know.

Because of the books.

Because of that mechanic, Randy.

Because of Glenda and Mr. Xavier, because of David Beckett and Pete. Because of that terrible summer when she was almost thirteen.

Afterward, the day the vice principal's letter came, her father stood before her. He seemed, momentarily, to shrink while the white and yellow patterned wallpaper leaped out at her, and through the living room window she saw heat waves rising from the roof of a car outside.

Then she seemed to shrink and her father expanded. His head was large and round, his arms heavy and long at his sides.

"Daddy," she whispered. She loved him—didn't she still? He used to tickle her and bounce her on his lap. "Who's Daddy's sweetheart? Where'd this little baby come from?" He would blow against the side of her neck to make her laugh and laugh.

He had taught her to answer, "From the cabbage patch!"

"Right from the cabbage patch!" Gleefully he would tickle and kiss again.

Now he said, *"What did you do?"* Each word stood separately.

"Look, Daddy." Claudia moistened her lips. Smog had settled in her throat.

"What did you do?"

"I protested."

"What did you protest?"

"The rule. The idea that boys and girls have to be treated differently. It's discriminatory, Daddy!"

"Discriminatory? For boys and girls to dress differently? Are you crazy?"

"It is, Dad! Glenda French was telling us about past discrimination—against blacks and Catholics and foreigners—people used to take it for granted. Like slavery. Who protested slavery back then? Only a few people. But now—everybody knows it's wrong. Today things are happening exactly like—"

"What the hell are you telling me?"

"It's a cultural thing, Daddy. There is nothing wrong, nothing inherently private about the female . . . look, in Tahiti none of the women wear . . ."

He only stared at her. "So it's true," he said at last. He looked old, his cheeks sagging, though his mouth was clenched. "You sat there in the schoolyard. In the bleachers. And in front of the whole student body you took off your . . ."

He swallowed, stared. "You took off . . ."

He looked at the wallpaper. "You exposed your breasts. Completely."

"Dad. Listen. I know it sounds—"

"And you continued to sit there. And when you were asked to cover yourself, you became defiant."

"You don't understand." The words sounded hollow. She whispered, "You have to have been there."

"If I had been there," he said, "I would have killed you."

For the first time in her life he struck her across the face, a staggering blow.

6

Afterwards I tried to reconstruct it. But I couldn't. There are some things you can't explain.

On Monday, Mr. Xavier lectured us about power. How in this country you have to be a man to have power. You have to be white. And it helps if you're Protestant. He talked about corruption. Hypocrisy. Somehow, it hurt. And I wasn't the only one. People left class silently, subdued. The heat wave had already begun. My eyes and throat ached from the smog.

Mr. Xavier's lecture hung in my mind all day and through the night. Tuesday, the moment I woke up I could smell the pollution. I was tired. For days I'd been reading, thinking, wrestling with questions I couldn't quite put into words. I'd wanted to talk to my friends over the weekend, but they were busy. I called Scott long distance at college, but he sounded funny and finally told me he had a "guest" in his room.

Tuesday was a bummer from the beginning. I had nothing to wear. All my summer clothes were packed away. So I wore white denims and a loose blue cotton workshirt, thinking the long sleeves would shield me from the hot sun.

It started first thing in journalism.

Greg Furrier (we call him Furry or Fur Face) makes out the assignments. It's been a hassle all term. He's weird. He had Denise Hunter doing all the school board meetings which is the worst assignment in the world. He made Sylvia Getz do a piece about that rock group, The Planet Seven, knowing full well that Sylvia is the only person in the school who when you say "concert" thinks you mean the philharmonic.

So, naturally, Furry assigned yours truly to cover the Tuesday afternoon swim meet. That's Joey Armata's usual beat. He gave Joey a movie review.

I tried to resist. "I know beans about swim meets."

Furry grinned. "So, then write about beans."

"Please. Let me do tennis instead. Or the movie. Anything!"

"A reporter," said Furry, "must be flexible."

I appealed to Miss Merriman. She shrugged and said, as usual, "I am only the advisor. Editorial decisions are made by the student staff."

"It isn't fair!" I objected.

"Life isn't fair," she said. Then she clamped her mouth shut and returned to editing copy.

So I dragged myself through the day, dreading the afternoon and that swim meet. I hate the smell of chlorine and sitting in those hot bleachers. During P.E., I persuaded Vivian to come with me.

It was so hot we left our hair dripping wet. Vivian decided to wear her gym clothes the rest of the day. I just took off my bra and stuck it in my backpack and rolled up my cuffs and sleeves.

My mother thinks it's obscene not to wear a bra. Later, it was one of the things she harped about.

Fifth period, I was thrilled to see Glenda French in Mr. Xavier's class. She smiled at me and nodded, like a signal. I smiled back. After class I'd go and talk to her. We'd talk about those books. She'd understand. In some deep way we were the same. I knew exactly why she had gone into law. Why she was so caught up with civil rights and discrimination. She began to speak, and I could almost see myself standing in her place.

It was Glenda's day. Glenda's lesson. We were all fascinated. She spoke brilliantly about the struggle. About men and women and laws. The inequities. The cruel discrimination.

Somehow she got us going. The class came alive. Kids who had never spoken out before now argued, shouted, interrupted in their excitement. Back and forth the arguments raged, our voices blending and overlapping . . .

"It's society that makes women feel inferior."

"Women are weaker."

"They don't really want to make their own decisions."

"No, it's their training, and what's expected of them."

"Shouldn't women get paid the same as men for the same work?"

Then, of course, it got nasty and illogical. People yelled out, jeering, until gradually the mass frenzy worked itself down to just a few voices. Mine was among them.

I was not afraid to speak. The words I'd read all weekend came leaping to my lips, perfect and clear. For the first time I possessed power and authority. I knew this subject better than any of them! I began.

"The whole point is really economic power," I stated. "Who controls the money. Who makes all the major decisions."

"My mother!" shrieked Aldo Sullivan; and Julian, Bob and David Beckett roared with appreciative laughter.

Marsha McClure joined me, her eyes narrowed. "That's the old line," she said. "Men like to make women think they have control, when all they really get to decide is what brand of soap to buy."

Boys whooped and laughed.

"That's right," I said. "Look at the commercials. Daddy builds highways or goes to a terrific office downtown. Mom sits and worries about how to remove rings around the collar. Isn't that telling us something?"

"Yeah!" yelled Aldo. "We all got dirty necks!"

They screamed with laughted, and I stood up to face them. "You make jokes when we're being serious! It's a cop-out."

Marsha took up the fight, standing at her place. "We resent it," she cried. "We were quiet till now . . ."

"Oho! Quiet?"

"It's not funny," I said, "when half the people put down the other half. It's like—like a kind of slavery. In some states women can't even own property. They get stiffer penalties for the same crimes. Advertising is just a symbol."

"Then why," said David Beckett firmly, logically, "do you babes fall for all that junk?"

"Where do you get off calling us babes?" yelled Marsha. "You're a turd!"

"Let's keep this impersonal," murmured Mr. Xavier.

"You won't stay on the issue," I cried. "That's what we're talking about. Everything is geared to keep women off balance, insecure, out of power."

"If you've got no economic power," said David, "why would they aim all the ads at you?"

I felt as if I'd been slapped. Heat rose in waves around me. I didn't want to argue against David. I didn't want to fight him—David, David. Part of me would always love him.

Heavily I said, "The real power has nothing to do with that. That's small stuff. The point is, women are kept out of the big decisions. Like . . ."

"Treaties," supplied Marsha.

"Treaties," I echoed. "And being presidents of big companies. Or in government. Women don't decide to build rockets or buy missiles. Men do that. They have the power to destroy the world. And they're just about doing it."

Everyone tensed. I could feel it. Now the room was silent. It was between David and me.

David stood up. "Come on," he said. He laid back his head, grinning, and in that moment I wanted to slap him, hard. "Do you really want to carry a rifle?" His voice was smooth, mocking. "Is that what you want? You want to be in the army?"

"No! We want the equal right to decide that maybe there won't be an army. Maybe there won't be any more war. Men have been working at this for over five thousand years. They've made one big bloody mess of it!"

Girls stamped and cheered and roared approval. I was borne up in it, dizzy, exhilarated, strong. I stepped closer toward David. I spoke loudly, distinctly. I gave him facts.

He remained cool. Only his eyes changed. They were dark with the heat of this battle.

"As far as I'm concerned," he said, "you may have the right to get yourself killed. But the point is, you keep *complaining*, about women being *pressured*." He drew out the words. "If you can't take the pressure, you don't really belong up there making decisions."

"Being sensitive doesn't mean we can't take it—"

He interrupted. "But you do agree that men and women are different," he said.

"Different, yes!" I cried. "But equal. With the same rights."

"Oh. Pardon me. I thought I heard you talking about us being the same. And, honestly, I can't help noticing that in certain very terrific ways you are entirely different from me!"

Boys whistled and screamed. I felt my face get hot and red; I wanted to crawl under the seat, to vanish.

David, striding toward me, pressed on. "Of course, I say, *vive la différence!*"

"Sex has nothing to do with it," I managed to say.

"Sex has everything to do with it!" David shouted. He gestured like an orator. "Women just want everything handed to them on a silver platter. They want rights, but they don't want to work for them. Glenda French told us that no group ever won their rights without a struggle. She told us how people were willing to put their lives on the line for what they believe. But women have never wanted to make any sacrifices . . ."

"Why should we sacrifice?" I cried, aghast.

"Women use sex to get what they want. That's all they've ever done. We all know it."

That did it. Everything blew apart.

It took until the bell rang for Mr. Xavier and Glenda to restore order.

Finally Mr. Xavier called out, "Claudia Warner is right in pointing out the exploitation of women. David Beckett is correct in reminding us that women need to *act* on their ideals." He smiled and waved. "Good class!"

I hated David Beckett.

Vivian knew right away.

"What's wrong?"

I told her briefly. It was stupid. I was shaking. How had I gotten involved in this whole dumb thing?

"Don't worry about it," said Vivian. She got a program, handed it to me as we got to the bleachers. "Here. You'll need this to write your story."

"Thanks." Already the blare of the loudspeaker and the smell of chlorine were getting to me.

I hadn't attended a swim meet since my freshman year. Now I remembered why.

Marsha McClure sat with some other girls a few rows away. She waved and smiled. I tried to smile back, but I felt miserable. I have a free sixth period; all hour I'd rehashed what happened between me and David Becket, getting hotter and madder.

The song girls ran down in front of the cheering section, where all the rah-rah's sit. The rah-rah's wear yellow flowers on their wrists and buy those huge, awful yellow cookies to raise money for the teams.

I felt out of it. I thought of writing a mean parody. I couldn't stand any of them, the cheerleader, the girls with their little yellow skirts and the blue ruffled panties underneath. I hated the way they baby-talked. "Whee-whee, Menominee!" Then they'd turn and stoop to show their ruffles.

I scanned the program. Coach Purcell, with the whistle around his neck, was talking earnestly to Hiram Fox.

"Maybe I'll just interview Hiram," I said.

"Good idea." Vivian nodded and smiled to soothe me.

All right. I'd cover the story. Do a decent job on it. Forget David Beckett and Xavier's class.

The song girls bounced and giggled and stooped.

Someone blasted a horn. It sounded like New Year's Eve. People screamed with laughter and started to throw things.

"Cut it out, you guys!"

"What a bunch of apes."

"Hear it for Menominee—whee-whee, Menominee!"

"Would you guys cut it out?" Vivian called as an empty soda pop can landed beside us. "You're so juvenile."

Two rows down from us sat Aldo Sullivan with Julian Margolis and another guy, named Dillon.

The yelling filled all the space like melting rubber or liquid plastic. I saw David Beckett come down from the top of the bleachers to join his friends.

Splashing. Streaks of flesh. Smell of chlorine.

"There's David Beckett," whispered Vivian.

"I saw."

They started acting like idiots. As if they owned the place. You know how guys can get at a game. Laughing and pushing and yelling. They stood up and blocked our view. They slapped each other's backs, waved their arms.

Names were called on the loudspeaker.

The coach blew his whistle.

Four bodies hit the water with a splash, a roar of cheers.

"So hot my pants are fried!"

"Move over, you moose."

"Too hot for clothes."

"Take 'em off!"

"Whew! Is your deodorant fail safe?"

The boys took off their shirts. Their bodies were bronze in the sun. They sat with their heads thrown back, contented as seals sunning themselves on rocks. Sweat gleamed on David Beckett's back. I was awed by the rippling of his muscles and by the feelings that still claimed me. I had never felt this way with Pete. Never.

Vivian murmured, "He's got a terrific build."

Her voice was lost in a swell of cheering. Somebody obviously broke a record. I sat amid the commotion, clutching my notebook, aware that I wanted him—wanted him terribly, while still I hated him for humiliating me and for his superior tone, his arrogance. All those things in him that were male, these I wanted, these I resented. The heat and the crowd seemed to close in on me. Again, it all subsided. The people sat down. Soon the boys called out again, poked at each other, showing off.

Somehow their comments became directed at us. They started to bug us. Before I knew it we were yelling back.

"Shut up, Dillon!"

"Oh, yeah, the lady's working. She's a big-shot reporter."

"Why don't you guys sit down so we can see?"

"She'll do a bad write-up anyway. What does she know?"

"Hey, move over, you freaks!"

"Hey, Claudia, you gonna write about us?"

Someone threw a paper cup from above. It hit me across the cheek. The sting was sharp, unexpected.

"Who did that?" I yelled, glancing around.

"Who did that?" they mimicked.

I felt tears starting, as if I'd been really hurt, a slap.

". . . should have heard that lady lawyer in our class . . . I'd like to get her alone in . . ." The words swelled into the commotion from the swimming pool, ". . . and get some of that pitch out of her . . . hot stuff."

They laughed, clapped each other on the back, pushed and shoved.

". . . if she's so equal, she ought to prove it."

And suddenly, somehow, I was involved, Aldo Sullivan yelling up at me, "Hey, Claudia, do you think if that Glenda dame was here she'd take her top off? It's only natural, you know."

The boys were pawing at each other, convulsed with laughter.

"What a trip she is!"

"Listen, all they want is equal. Ain't that right? Everything the same."

"She says you gotta test the law. Isn't that what she said, Claudia?"

They were screaming my name. My cheeks burned.

"Big lawyer. Hey, *is* there a law against girls taking off their shirts?"

"Didn't you hear that lady lawyer? She says it's unconstitutional unless everything is equal, exactly the same."

"She said that?"

Vivian bent to me. "Let's move," she said.

"No." The feeling had already seized me, was building in me. "No," I said. "We were here first."

"But they're being gross."

"Then let them move," I said.

". . . she says . . . that dumb dame . . . why

44

doesn't she . . . hey, why don't you just go ahead and prove . . ."

"Leave her alone." It was David Beckett, loud and bossy, coming to my defense. As if I needed him.

That was what did it.

I stood up.

"What's wrong, Claudia?"

I glimpsed Vivian's frown. Then her mouth slowly shaped an "O," everything moving in slow motion, my own hands feeling thick and strange as I unbuttoned my shirt, pulled it off and stood there feeling the hot sun on my flesh.

I don't know how long I stood there. Things melted together. Sounds were muted and faces blurred. I might have been floating above the scene in a ballon, except that I also knew exactly what I was doing, part of me urging, Do it! Do it!

No reasons, questions or doubts. Only this. Standing nude to the waist with the hot sun on my skin. Rejoicing. Free.

Dimly I heard Vivian call my name. Someone grabbed my shirt away. Marsha McClue and her three friends yanked off their tops, flung them away, and I heard them screaming at the top of their lungs, "All right! That'll show 'em! Male chauvinist pigs! Male chauvinist pigs!"

The glare of horns and the booming from the loudspeaker rose to a crescendo as Coach Purcell approached.

7

Coach Purcell came running up the bleachers. His voice was cool and casual, but tension lines showed around his mouth. "All right, girls. Put your shirts back on."

Claudia stood motionless. The sun beat against her body. Dimly she saw Coach Purcell bend down and look around. Marsha and her friends had covered themselves and fled.

"Where the heck is your shirt?" Coach Purcell demanded. He was edgy now; no telling what might happen.

From far off Claudia heard a commotion. Closer by, a deep silence, like a dream.

Coach Purcell ducked down, looking under the seats. Her shirt fluttered past, was caught in an impromptu game of keep away. The coach grabbed a boy's arm and commanded, "George, go get me a blanket."

The boy's face went beet red.

"Listen." Sweat streaked the coach's face. "What's your name?" He looked at the notebook on the bench. "Claudia. Listen. I don't know why you're doing this. I—I'm sure you have reasons. But—uh—uh I'm afraid you're going to be very embarrassed later on. Listen . . ."

Claudia felt oddly like a diver on the high board, afraid to move, afraid to stay. She did not look at the coach.

Then a thick blanket was laid around her shoulders. Coach Purcell held his arm around her back, urging her down past the students, girls with glittering, astonished eyes, boys whooping or silently staring—past the flash of David Beckett's blue eyes, down to the concrete where the swimmers toed the edge of the pool.

Suddenly everything seemed to tear loose.

Objects hit the air. Tennis shoes, soda pop cans, books, bags and paper boxes—everything came hurtling down, plus a couple of bottles, which hit the pavement with a crash. Now amid the crazy hooting and gleeful hollering, people began to scream in real panic. They ducked under benches. Some shielded their heads with books. The mob whirled and yelled, "Atta way, baby! Let it all hang out!"

People pushed, fell, ran, while the voice over the loudspeaker boomed out like a disembodied spirit, "Students! Settle down. Take your seats. Go back to your seats!"

The band struck up with a feeble chorus of "Home to Menominee." The song girls were pulled into action. "Whee, whee, Menominee!" And Claudia was led away.

She found herself in the office on a hard chair, holding the blanket so tightly her hands felt numb. Still, she shivered.

"Dr. Wallenburg is away at a conference," Coach Purcell said with a nervous cough. "So Mr. Milden will . . ."

At that moment Mr. Milden entered, his tread heavy and precise, almost military. The students called him "Mildew." They said he smelled of it. Claudia didn't know. She had never been that close to the vice principal. One saw him stalking the campus, pale and intense.

The two men spoke; low rumbling sounds reached Claudia as through a tunnel.

". . . some of the kids got a little carried away. It's been so hot."

"So you let them go nude? What's the . . . ?"

Purcell's voice continued, soothing, reasonable.

Beside it Mr. Milden's words made staccato bursts, clipped and angry. ". . . this whole permissive attitude! Think they'd have more self-respect . . . getting away with murder. *Literally, murder.*"

"Well, this girl seems fairly . . ." Coach Purcell's voice faded, rose again. ". . . a little extreme."

"Settle this here and now. Here and now, do you understand?"

Cave Milden approached. Claudia could see his shoes moving toward her.

He asked, "Is she on drugs?"

Claudia whispered, "No. I don't take drugs."

"Claudia Warner. Look at me."

Claudia moved her eyes to his face. Her head buzzed and ached.

"I suppose you have an explanation for what is going on here."

"I—no."

"Things have a way of escalating," offered Coach Purcell.

"Did you ask this young woman to clothe herself?"

"Actually, I believe she was in—shock."

"I should think so! *I* find her behavior shocking. And disgusting."

Coach Purcell coughed slightly.

"Since you're not on drugs," stated Cave Milden, "we know you are fully aware of your actions. That means you must take full responsibility for them."

Claudia shivered.

"Now, you will tell me the names of all the other participants in this little demonstration."

Claudia said nothing. Whatever had happened, it no longer seemed part of her. She only wanted to go home, to

48

sleep. Faintly she whispered. "I'm sorry. I want to go home."

"You will tell me their *names*. Then you may go home. I don't think you understand the seriousness of your situation. Indecent exposure. Inciting a riot. Conspiring—"

"Actually, I don't think Claudia intended—"

"Disciplinary measures will be taken!" Milden shouted, drawing himself upright, wincing, as in pain.

At that moment came a sound like distant waves, moving closer. Milden rushed to the window. The sound rose, and he stepped back from it, astounded, confronting some thirty or forty students, mostly boys. For them, it had all ended too quickly. They wanted more.

> "Hey! Hey!
> Let her stay,
> We don't see this every day!"

They spread out, shouting and laughing. The heat, the boredom, the promise of excitement so swiftly ended, all combined to stir them up, and they chanted in a frenzy, dancing about:

> "Hey! Hey!
> Let her stay!
> Let her go!
> All the way!
> All the way!
> All the WAY!"

Cave Milden gathered his rage. He gripped the window-sill and shouted out, "Disperse! I order you to disperse at once. In ten seconds, I promise you, I will call the police."

He stood. He counted. "Ten. Nine. Eight . . ."

The students fell silent in disbelief. All this seemed

handed down from another place, another time—they were just goofing off. It was all so *stupid*.

". . . two. One."

Cave Milden made sure they saw him from the window as simultaneously he reached for the telephone and rang three bells for the security agent, Bates.

Someone let out a howl. Someone threw a trash can over on its side. The garbage can lid came flying through the air like an enormous Frisbie. It glanced off the window, where instantly a long, crooked crack appeared. Now the din was different. Trash cans were thrown, kicked, made into weapons. Boys seemed to change into grim-fraced men, men needing battle.

In the next moment Coach Purcell ran out and stood among them, blasting his whistle. Blast! Blast! A trash can lid scudded along the ground. It struck him on the calf. He recoiled from the pain, quickly straightened and called out, "All right! Look, the party's over. Listen. Listen a minute!" His voice dropped to a moderate, reasonable tone. "I think we're all a little crazy from the heat. There's a girl in there who's had a pretty rough day. Now, let's just let it go at that."

Two minutes later, when security agent Bates arrived, the yard was empty. Cave Milden's face was pinched, almost gray.

"I want a full report on the damage," he said. His gaze was fixed just above Claudia's head. "I will personally see to it that her parents pay every penny of the damages."

"Just some litter, Mr. Milden," said the coach, wiping his face.

"And this crack in the window."

Claudia said distinctly, "I didn't break that window." It felt, strangely, as if someone else were speaking through her.

The next moment she was yanked forward so violently

that her arm felt wrenched at the shoulder. The blanket fell away; swiftly she clutched it over her breast, sobbing.

"Now you will tell me the names of the others!" shouted Milden. "Now! Now!"

But it was too late. Claudia shook her head. No more tears. No more *anything*.

Cave Milden walked around his desk and sat down. He jerked open the drawer. He took out a pink slip, wrote swiftly on it. "Claudia Warner. You are suspended from school for three days. Should you appear on this campus, I promise you, I will have you expelled. And you will pay for this. Make no mistake."

The telephone rang. Cave Milden picked it up, standing ramrod straight. Only his face indicated his changing emotions as he spoke.

"*The Shore Times*? Yes. A reporter? How in the world . . . of course I'll have a statement. I can promise you that the young lady involved will be severely . . ."

Like a sleepwalker, Claudia moved out, letting the office door close on the rest of Mr. Milden's comment.

8

It was like waking up in the morning and seeing a different face in the mirror. She had thought she knew herself. She didn't.

By a stroke of luck, her parents were going out for the evening—some insurance convention in town. Otherwise, her mother might have noticed that something was wrong. Claudia could never quite figure out how her mother perceived such things, but then, it was mutual.

Claudia telephoned Vivian and Bennie. Both of them came right after dinner. Having them here in her room took away some of the fear and dread she had felt since this afternoon.

"You guys," she began, nearly crying, "you're great to come. I really needed you. I feel like the biggest jerk in the world."

"My mother thought the whole thing was hilarious," said Vivian. "When she was a kid she was always into trouble."

Bennie gasped. "You told your mother about it?"

"Sure." Vivian grinned. "She asked if I did it too. I almost think she's disappointed that I'm not a rebel. You know, into politics and campaigns instead of football games and boys. She thinks Yale is *terribly conventional*. Her words."

"If I ever did anything like that," Bennie said flatly, "my parents would ground me for a year."

"They don't have to worry," said Vivian. "You're such a good little girl."

"Lay off!" Bennie shook her head. "I just couldn't do that. I'd die."

"I did it," Claudia said wryly. "Nobody died."

"But they started a riot."

"You call that a riot?" Vivian lay back, cool, sipping cola from a can. "A few kids got worked up. They were just looking for an excuse."

"They'll say Claudia triggered it."

Claudia stared at her. "Whose side are you on, Bennie?"

Bennie's cheeks were red with splotches, as always when she was upset.

"I'm not condemning you, Claudia," Bennie said softly. "I respect you for taking a stand. But people will say—"

"Who cares about other people?" Vivian cried. "You have to do what you think is right!"

"But what made it right?" demanded Bennie.

"I told you! The boys were bugging us," Vivian said. "They were acting so superior. You know how they get."

"That's why Claudia took her top off?"

"You have to have been there, Bennie."

Bennie twisted her hands, turning away. "Other people," she persisted, "will say it's against the law to take off your top in public. They'll say it's obscene."

"Now, see?" Claudia's eyes blazed as she turned to Vivian. "My best friend thinks I'm obscene. How can I ever go back to school if people—"

"Forget it!" cried Vivian. "Look, nobody saw anything today they wouldn't see in any art gallery. Or an "R" movie. Good grief, there's a nude beach down at the Point.

My mom told me the women in France always swim topless. What's the big deal?"

"It doesn't matter what they do in France," Claudia said dully. "You see why I can't go back to school."

"Listen, by Monday everybody will have forgotten about it. It'll be history. Like the "L" Club stealing Bob's Big Boy. Or that guy six years ago who went BA in the yearbook."

"Well, you still remember that," Claudia snapped.

"True," nodded Vivian. "But nobody condemns those guys. You're too sensitive."

"You'll be a legend," added Bennie, conciliatory.

"Thanks a bunch. That's terrific."

"For the next three days," said Vivian, "just go to the beach or the mall. Your folks will never even know you were suspended."

"Don't they send a note home?" Bennie asked.

"No," said Vivian. She took a sip of cola. "That's just when you're expelled."

"Tomorrow's my mom's monthly sales meeting," Claudia said. "That means she'll be out all day."

"There. You see? Everything will work out. You just have to cool it."

The telephone rang. It was Yale, looking for Vivian.

Vivian got that look in her eyes and settled deep into the seat, smiling.

"Really?" she squeezed her eyes shut. "No, we didn't see a thing. They did?" She gestured broadly, noiselessly grinning. "No kidding! Wow. Who was it? Hey, listen, I've gotta go. Yeah. Sure. Ten minutes."

She hung up, rolled her eyes and shrieked. "What a blast! You won't believe this. You'll die. That was Yale."

"You don't say."

"Listen! Listen!" Vivian yelled. "He wanted to know if I knew who those girls were minus their tops at the swim meet! Can you imagine! He says he heard this rumor, but nobody knows the girls' names. Isn't that a blast?"

"Show's you how popular I am," said Claudia with a groan.

"This place is a zoo," said Bennie. "I can't wait to graduate."

"It proves I was right!" exclaimed Vivian. "Nobody cares. Nobody even knows it was you. So there's nothing to get yourself all spaced out about."

Outside a horn sounded. Vivian leaped up. "That's Yale. Bennie, do you need a ride home?" She looked so worried that Claudia and Bennie both burst out laughing.

"I wouldn't dream of intruding," said Bennie with a grin. "I'll call my brother."

While she waited, Bennie fixed her lip gloss, brushed her hair, sighing deeply.

"What's wrong?" Claudia went to her.

Bennie looked at her through the mirror. "I wish I could understand it."

"Some things," said Claudia, "can't be explained. You just do what you have to do. I had to make David Beckett choke on his words. Show him I wasn't going to take that from him anymore."

"You're still in love with him."

"I love him, and I can't stand him, too. But that's not the reason. I just couldn't let him win!"

"What if it hadn't been David, but some other boy?"

"I don't know. You should read some of these books."

"Books don't always tell you the truth," said Bennie.

Claudia picked up one of them, thumbed through the pages. "Listen." She read: "An old Moslem proverb about women says, 'When a man has a precious jewel, it's wiser to lock it up in a box than leave it about for anyone to take.'"

"What's that supposed to prove?"

"That the woman is a possession. Like a jewel."

Bennie gazed at herself in the mirror. "I never felt that I was locked up in a box," she said.

"You're lucky."

The next morning, when her mother came in to wake her, Claudia turned her face into the pillow. "I'm not feeling well. Staying home today."

Her mother, as always on sales meeting days, was cheery and preoccupied, dressed in her good suit with the silk print blouse and several gold bangles on her arm. "Well, all right, dear. I have to leave. Take it easy. Can I get you anything?"

Claudia wanted to cry out, "Mom! Mom!" and have her mother come and sit on the bed, put her cool hand on Claudia's cheek, maybe even hold her.

"No," Claudia said.

After a moment her mother added, "Be sure to let the cat out later."

Claudia had had a dream. She had just given birth to a baby. A baby! A large black woman with pendulous breasts came to her, holding out the infant. "Don't you want your child? Here, take this little child. You birthed it. Don't you want this child?"

Her grandfather used to say dreams have deep meanings. All Claudia could think of was that single word—suspended. It hissed in her mind. Suspended. Curious word, it meant something hanging in midair. Unresolved. Well, as long as her parents didn't find out . . .

She pulled on her jeans and shirt and, barefoot, stepped outside the kitchen door to smell the day. No smog. Glory be. Clear air and cooler.

Well, there might be consequences to what she had done yesterday. Maybe the suspension would go on her record. Or her parents might find out about it somehow. All right. Her dad would ground her. It would be worth it. She had stood up to Cave Milden.

Claudia picked up *The Shore Times*. She took it inside, remembering her own story of the swim meet and tomorrow's deadline. Murder! OK. She'd write it up. Send it over with Bennie tomorrow. No sweat.

Idly she began to turn the pages of *The Shore Times*. Then it struck her.

HOT COED DOFFS TOP AT SCHOOL SWIM MEET. SPURS RIOT.

It was like a nightmare.

The photograph was fuzzy, and black lines shielded the pertinent places. Her name was not here, but still . . . HOT COED. If one could die of embarrassment, it would happen now. How could they print it? By what right?

She could hardly read the article, for the shock had made her numb, her eyes almost refusing to focus. At last the words came.

". . . the young woman was covered with a blanket and led away while teachers tried to subdue the hundreds of screaming, rioting students. Within an hour, according to Cave Milden, vice-principal, nearly a dozen irate parents telephoned the school in protest. Mr. Milden assured parents that, 'Lawlessness and vulgar behavior will not be tolerated at Menominee High School.'"

The telephone rang. Sylvia Getz.

"Have you seen *The Shore Times*?"

"Just now."

"You'd better get over here."

"I'm grounded. Suspended."

"Oh, my God. Listen. People are going ape around here. I think you should tell your side of the story."

"There's no story, Sylvia."

"Oh, yes there is. We have to respond to that piece in *The Shore Times*. You know that. Some people here want to string you up."

"Who?"

"Dear little Denise Hunt. Everybody's sweetie pie. She's about to get her claws in your back."

It took seven minutes flat for Claudia to bicycle down to the high school. She swerved at the open door of "Publications," left her bike beside the path and moved toward the turmoil.

Greg Furrier sat atop a desk, gesturing grandly. "We've obviously got a kind of protest here. A student is making a *statement*."

"It's just a cheap bid for attention," said Denise Hunt, her eyes flashing. "I think we should expose it for what it is."

"Expose!" screamed Joey Armata, arms waving and giggling. "Ha—good one! Pun! Ha-ha-ha."

From the typesetting machine Miss Merriman murmured, "Settle down, students."

Claudia, standing just behind the doorway, felt a peculiar sense of being invisible.

"Let's stick to the issues," said Hank Tillman, the editor, leaning against the file cabinet.

"Denise Hunt is overreacting," snapped Sylvia Getz; usually gentle, she pointed now at Denise in anger.

"The issue," persisted Hank, "is whether the school has the right to tell students how to dress." He allowed himself a slight smile. "Or not to dress."

Only Joey Armata laughed.

"Second," said Hank, "and I suppose this is the basic issue, can the dress code be different for boys than for girls?"

It unleashed a small storm as people shouted.

"Of course it's different!"

"No—that would be unconstitutional."

"I see your point, Hank."

"Different is unequal, no matter what."

"Then what about sports? We don't have coed wrestling."

Miss Merriman took a single step away from the machine. "All these issues," she said, "should be discussed in editorials. This is feature material, not news."

Denise Hunt stood up. Her face was red and puffy. "I think it sucks. It's . . ." She glanced at the teacher. ". . . outrageous. People do anything they want and get away with it by calling it a protest and an issue. Who wants to see people running around naked on campus?" She glanced around, challengingly. Even Joey Armata remained silent. "I certainly don't. I don't think it's just a matter of common decency!"

"Whose definition of decency?" screamed Sylvia. "Yours? I can certainly identify with the fact that Claudia took a stand."

"Maybe you identify! I don't. One girl does one dumb thing and right away everybody jumps up saying what a terrific statement it was. I don't think it takes a lot of courage to be a complete *jerk*. I think it was stupid. I'll bet ninety percent of the girls on this campus agree with me."

"We could take a poll," said Greg Furrier soberly.

"I think you're jealous," stated Sylvia.

"I think you're crazy," retorted Denise.

"Look, guys!" Hank Tillman rose to his full height of six feet, two inches. "It's obvious we'll have to run two pieces. Pro and con. Like we did on that draft piece."

"We should get a statement from Claudia Warner," said Greg.

"I'm here," Claudia said from the doorway.

Silence. The boy at the typewriter pecked a few more letters, then looked around, startled and self-conscious.

Denise Hunt turned beet red; she bent studiously over her notebook.

Miss Merriman's eyes glistened, but she said nothing.

Hank Tillman took command. "Furrier, you do the pro. Who wants to do the con?" Nobody spoke. "Look, a minute ago some of you were very vocal." He glanced at

Denise, shrugged. "OK. I'll assign Joey. You better work with Claudia."

At that moment the light shifted, made a slight flickering. It combined with sound and motion in a struggle so swift and so fierce that later many different versions survived.

Cave Milden, striding to the Publications room with his own rebuttal to *The Shore Times* article, saw Claudia Warner standing in the doorway in defiance of her suspension. He reached out, seized her. Some said he actually struck her. Others said she whirled around so fast that her head hit his jaw and he winced and shouted for the officer across the yard, "Bates! Bates!"

The security guard, still stinging from the rebuke over yesterday's episode, responded immediately.

"This student is here in defiance of suspension rules!" shouted Cave Milden. "Remove her from campus!"

In the melee and confusion, some said the security guard roughed her up. Others said he only took her arm. Several people claimed they saw him actually dragging Claudia off the campus, screaming.

g

"Still sick?" her mother asked on Thursday morning. "Kinda."

She did not know yet. Claudia had taken *The Shore Times* to the trash can and dumped the soiled kitty litter on top of it. Her mom praised her for cleaning out the litter box without being told.

"Well, you don't want to miss too much school." She seemed to notice Claudia for the first time in weeks. "You do look a little pale."

"Maybe I need some LovLee rouge," said Claudia, and her mother turned away with a helpless sigh.

That afternoon the letter came. Claudia was out on the hammock. Her mother called from the window. Like a little child, Claudia ran in. She knew immediately. In one hand Mom held the letter, in the other the envelope with the printed return address, "Menominee High School." Milden. The rat. Had notified her mother in writing; she did not know then that this was required in cases of suspension. Parents had to be notified and called in to a conference before the student could return to school.

". . . and you let me go for *two days* without knowing?"

"You were busy with your sales meeting."

Later that night it was her father's turn to explode.

Finally Claudia was alone in her bedroom. Chaucer had been evicted by her father, who had hunted the cat as though it were a killer beast. He had held it high in the doorway, then dropped it out into the darkness, so that Claudia watching from her window, was outraged at his cruelty.

Later, long after her parents were asleep. Claudia began to change her room. She took all the little story book dolls from the high shelf over her desk. Next, she gathered all the picture books and juvenile novels that had collected in her bookcase all these years. Atop her bureau were some two dozen miniatures, sweet little tea sets, tables and chairs, and a sewing machine so delicate and authentic that it even had a bit of real thread in the needle and the little wheel turned.

From the hall closet Claudia got a carton. She packed her picture books on the bottom, then carefully wrapped each doll and each miniature in a tissue and laid them away.

Finally she took the yellow, puffy spread off her bed, rolled it up and thrust it deep into her closet, behind the shoes. Her blue and white plaid blanket was fancy enough for her taste. She filled the empty shelves with magazines, library books and flute music. The music trophy she had won two years ago stood alone on the top shelf where the dolls had been.

Everything has its price; the words came to her as she lay on her bed surveying her room. Soon she would leave this room forever. And forever she would feel the force of her father's blow.

The next day at the conference he was like a different person. He smiled a fraternal smile at Cave Milden. He shook hands warmly with Dr. Wallenburg. She had returned from Chicago with a bad cold. She apologized for coughing, holding a white handkerchief to her lips.

Dr. Wallenburg had white hair. Until this moment Claudia had thought of her as old. Now it was apparent that adults would find her "striking," for her skin was beautifully smooth, her eyes large and dark, her face and bearing implying dignity and intelligence.

"Since Mr. Milden has the facts of this case," she said, stifling a cough, "I believe he should conduct this conference."

Everyone nodded. Claudia and her mother sat like twin dolls in matched chairs. Dr. Wallenburg and the two men faced each other. Early this morning Claudia's mother had told her to wear her beige cotton dress and panty hose. She herself wore a tan and white checked suit and her "company" expression, as though she were at a party, expecting to be served canapés from a silver tray.

The two men were curiously alike in the way they took possession of their seats. They smiled alike, and together they spoke about young people nowadays, punctuating their points with certain phrases, ". . . well, in my day . . ." and agreeing about the state of the younger generation.

". . . too many disruptive influences . . ."

". . . well, in my day we had to earn every penny . . ."

". . . the tripe offered on television . . ."

". . . general decline of standards, well, look at our courts, for instance!"

Mr. Milden's voice held no malice. He recited the facts. His voice took on an almost fatherly tone; he had a job to do. Education was his whole life. "I care very deeply," he said, his eyes keen.

Dr. Wallenburg summed it up. "In reviewing this case," she said, "I conclude that Mr. Milden's action was entirely appropriate. Claudia's action was very—disruptive. We cannot tolerate that kind of defiance of school rules, not to mention city and county regulations."

"Dr. Wallenburg," said her father, "nobody here believes that Claudia's action was permissible. Nobody."

Claudia felt as though she were in an airless chamber, suffocating.

"Things like this," said Mr. Milden heavily, "can get dangerously out of control. You know how it is. One youngster takes the reins—others quickly follow. These are dangerous times. A generation without standards, without limits . . ."

"We have received dozens of phone calls," said Dr. Wallenburg. She blew her nose gently. "This is a community where parents are concerned about such things. On the one hand we have to fight apathy. On the other"—she glanced about the room, shook her head with resignation—"we have to contend with groups like the Women's League Committee on Education. They are very vocal. Extremely—"

"Dedicated to education," added Cave Milden. "And concerned for today's youth."

"Yes." Everyone nodded. Everyone agreed.

Claudia felt her mind drifting; the three adults reminded her of video game figures moving across a screen, responding predictably—bleep! bleep! pow!

Suddenly she realized Dr. Wallenburg was speaking to her. "What about it, young lady?"

"Pardon me?" Claudia was startled.

"We all agree," said Dr. Wallenburg, "it's best to resolve this matter quickly and quietly. Number one, we want you to get back into school. Now, since you violated your suspension . . ."

"The Women's League," murmured Mr. Milden.

Dr. Wallenburg shot him a glance. "Yes. The Women's League has written to me requesting that this case be severely dealt with. Actually," she said, "they are pushing for Claudia's expulsion. They want to make her an example."

Bleep! Bleep! Pow!

". . . of course we wish to avoid that. Nothing would be served by extremism. We are not here to obey the dictates of the Women's League. Your daughter"—Dr. Wallenburg smiled at Claudia's parents—"is not a tool. She's an individual."

Her parents nodded. Claudia was holding her breath.

"In my position," said Dr. Wallenburg, "I have to be sensitive to all segments of the community. I want to be fair."

"We appreciate that," said Claudia's father.

"I'm going to ask for Claudia's assurance that there will be no further such incidents. Her suspension ends after today. I'm sure that Claudia has no intention of causing any further trouble."

"That's right," said her father.

"And our students will simmer down. There's a dance tonight. It'll give them all something else to think about. Of course, you won't be involved, Claudia. I'm sure you understand what social probation means."

"Social—probation? *I'm on social probation?*"

"Weren't you listening, Claudia?" Dr. Wallenburg exchanged a glance with Mr. and Mrs. Warner.

"What do you mean?" Claudia cried, bracing her hands against the chair. "What do you mean?"

"You violated your suspension, Claudia. You had to be bodily removed from this campus. At least thirty students witnessed that," explained Dr. Wallenburg, with Mr. Milden nodding soberly.

"Social probation?" Claudia gazed at each of them. All the warm and living parts of her body seemed to congeal. Her mother was frowning slightly. The others stared at her.

"Nobody gets social probation!" Claudia cried out. "Only for the worst, the most serious offense—nobody gets that! For taking drugs, maybe. For stealing. Last year at the prom—"

"Claudia," said Dr. Wallenburg, "we are talking about *you*. We are talking about *now*."

"Claudia," said her father, "if I were you I would—"

"People were taking drugs right at the prom!" Claudia cried. "Everyone knew it. People all talked about it. Monty Haddigan, the head cheerleader was involved—everyone knew but nobody ever did anything because . . . because Monty Haddigan was a—"

"Sit down, Claudia," said her mother, for Claudia had risen to her feet and stood apart from them all.

"And one boy got his picture in the yearbook with his bare—"

"Sit down, Claudia!" her father commanded, looking himself again, strained and frantic.

"You don't seem to understand, Claudia," said Dr. Wallenburg. Her voice was calm and deliberate. "This administration is actually within its rights to expel you. Any student who causes disruption of the educational process, especially after having been warned . . ."

"Dr. Wallenburg, she doesn't usually behave like this. I—I assure you . . ."

"Walter, this is terrible . . ."

"Mr. Warner, I think when Claudia has had a chance to consider . . ."

If anyone had stood in Claudia's path, she would have knocked them down, so furiously did she run out of the office, leaving them with their gaping jaws and startled eyes.

10

Like an alien at her own school, Claudia kept herself camouflaged, wandering out by the gym, then to the eastern edge of campus where the thick hedge hugged the wall that the smokers and the stoners used for rendezvous. During the passing bells she felt the flow of students all about her, but she was still apart. She stood for a long time outside Mr. Xavier's classroom, her body pressed against the cold stucco, imagining that she felt the vibrations of his voice, longing to see him. But when the next bell rang students clustered all around him, and once again she fled.

In the lunch line she at last found Vivian and told her about the conference. They moved to the far end of the yard, where a small pile of beer cans lay half covered by dirt.

"I never heard of anything like it," Vivian said. Her voice was heavy with anger. "Nobody gets social probation except for committing a real *crime*. Remember last year, Peggy Hahn and Jordan Baker got social probation, but they were so drunk at the basketball game that they threw up on the floor."

"Then there was that boy who broke into the English

office in our freshman year and stole that test. Didn't he get social probation?"

"What's more important is who *didn't* ever get it—and should have. Like Monty Haddigan." Vivian sighed as she absent-mindedly proceeded to take her sandwich apart, crumb by crumb.

"I'm starving," Claudia told her, surprised to realize it was true.

Wordlessly Vivian handed her the battered sandwich. "Be my guest," she said gloomily.

"I feel like leaving," said Claudia. "For keeps."

"Have you seen the school paper?"

"No. I've been—" She snorted. "Busy."

"Denise Hunt, sweet Denise, really did a number on you." Vivian took the newspaper out of her notebook, held it out.

"Read it to me," said Claudia, eyes closed against the sun.

"'Most of the girls on this campus are shocked and embarrassed by the behavior of this female student who . . .'"

Claudia clamped her teeth together. Sweet Denise—everyone said she was so sweet.

"'. . . we see her behavior as a mere bid for attention. Students do not have the right to express themselves in ways that injure or disturb others. In the ensuing riot . . .'"

"Riot!" Claudia exclaimed. "She calls it a riot?"

"'. . . riot, several people were injured.'"

"That's a dirty lie!"

"'. . . trash was thrown into the swimming pool . . .'"

"She never even tried to get my side of it!" Claudia exclaimed. "She could have phoned me. Do you know, when Denise ran for treasurer she had me posting signs for her all over the school."

"She's a real fink," said Vivian. "Has to be the center of attention all the time. She's just jealous."

"Jealous! Come on, Vivian."

"She doesn't really have anything she didn't—"

"Oh, no—just great looks and a darling boyfriend and the cutest clothes . . ."

"Nothing she can't buy," said Vivian. "*You've* got talent."

"Oh, sure. Claudia, the great orator. You should have heard me against David Beckett."

"You're terrific on the flute."

"Vivian, they won't even let me play for the senior show."

"What?"

"Senior show is a social activity. I'm on social probation, remember?"

"But you've been rehearsing that piece for months! It isn't fair!"

Claudia turned her face away. This was something she hadn't wanted to think about. It wasn't doing the solo that mattered so much, but the piece itself. Her music teacher, Mrs. Seymour, had composed it. After seven years with a music teacher, there was a certain bond. People who didn't study music couldn't understand that, perhaps, but in a quiet, special way they had shared many things. There had been times when only Mrs. Seymour could help her.

"Then let's play, Claudia!" she would say briskly. "Music heals. Music helps. Every single day of your life should have some music in it."

Somehow, with Mrs. Seymour, it had been possible to think of "every single day of your life" as a broad tapestry filled with lovely sights and sounds, just as Mrs. Seymour's house was filled with relics and music and hand-crafted things.

Vivian spoke. "Was it awful? With your folks, I mean?"

"Yes," Claudia whispered. She would go visit Mrs.

Seymour: the thought flashed upon her as it had many times since Mrs. Seymour's death last winter. Then she would remember, always with that awful feeling, that bitter-hard taste like a stone in her mouth.

"I think I loved that lady."

Vivian gave her a quizzical look. "By next week," she said, "it will all blow over."

"I don't know. Dr. Wallenburg was talking about this Women's League. They want me expelled."

"Nobody gets expelled just like that," said Vivian. "It's illegal. They have to have a big hearing and everything."

"Mildew might like that."

"Hearings are terrible publicity."

For whom? Claudia wanted to ask, but didn't.

It felt strange stalking the campus like this—apart, almost invisible. There was this odd fantasy of being in charge of it all, making everything happen. No more being herded by bells and rules—she stood apart.

In a way it was exhilarating. This was what Mr. Xavier had meant by his soaring descriptions of those few valiant people who dared to battle against the majority, who dared to defy established custom. *They are the builders, the risk-takers. They hear the beat of a different drummer—they teach us all a new tune. Are there enough of them to bring us to a just society?*

How his words had infected them all! A just society—it made one's breath almost stop, the way he said it—a *noble* society. That was one of his special words. She used it whenever she could. "You are a noble cat," she told Chaucer, and would laugh at her own silliness, still loving the word.

She saw him cross the parking lot. She called, "Mr. Xavier! Mr. Xavier!" and ran, filled with a surge of excitement. Of course he knew what had happened. He knew all such things, talked about them in class, made lessons of them. No bold act was too trivial for him to notice.

"Mr. Xavier! I'm sorry I wasn't in class," she panted. "You see, I—"

"It's all right, Claudia," he said, turning to wait for her. "They should get you for the track team!" he exclaimed, admiring her speed, and she laughed, feeling glad all over.

His eyes—she might positively drown in those eyes.

"They sent me a note from the office," he explained. "So I knew about your suspension." He paused, then said earnestly, "I'm sorry."

She was breathing heavily. From running—he would think it was only from running. "I—I guess I'm in terrible trouble. Last Tuesday, I—"

"I know about it," he said. "I even read about it in *The Shore Times*. Those reporters can certainly smell out a story, can't they."

Her face burned—he had seen that picture. Even though it was blurry and shielded with dark lines—oh, God! She felt mortified. Stalling she murmured, "Are they allowed to do that? Take my picture and everything?"

"I guess it's within their rights. That reporter was covering the swim meet—happened to get in on something good. Uh—er . . ." He stopped, embarrassed, his face flushed. Then he laughed slightly. "I mean—making such a fuss. Suspending you and everything."

"I don't care about that," she said heatedly. "Now they've put me on social probation. That means I can't go to any of the school functions. Not even the prom or graduation."

His brows lifted as he stood back, appraising her. "Do you really care about all that stuff? I somehow thought . . ."

"It's the principle!" she replied quickly.

"Ah, yes. Of course." He nodded, rubbed the back of his neck. "The principle of a thing is—quite different."

71

"The punishment isn't fair," she persisted.

"Life isn't always fair," he said.

"Then we have legal remedies!"

"Touché!" He laughed, but ruefully. "Nothing like getting it back from one of your own students!" Then he added, "You did violate a school rule."

"What rule?"

"Against nudity on campus."

"What about the boys? They were as nude as I!"

"Oh, Claudia, now you are getting into this whole sex discrimination thing, and that is a very complex area."

"But you said women have to—"

"Claudia. You have to take things with a little grain of salt. Obviously, there are inequities. And obviously, we want people to work for social change. But it has to be done in an orderly way, within the system."

Claudia blinked, as if the sun was too bright and beaming into her eyes, and his face jumping at her, teeth flashing. "But that day Glenda French came to class . . ."

"You see, Dr. Wallenburg already suspects that it was something in my class that triggered your—your outburst. That's Dr. Wallenburg's term for it."

"But you said women need to act out their ideals."

"I didn't mean for you to go around topless! My God, Claudia, a person has to use good judgment. If I told you to jump off the roof . . ."

"I'd probably do it," she said faintly, doubtful that he had heard it, realizing with a jolt that it was true. And did he even care?

"Now, my dear." His voice was suddenly soft. He led her to the low wall where they sat down together. She was so aware of his presence that she could hardly think. "You've got to understand," he said, "that this is a very sensitive issue."

Sensitive. Her mind held the word.

"People get very uptight about such things. I realize it's

unfair to you. These things get very—political. Do you know what I mean?"

She nodded. She gazed at the outline of his lips, could feel his breathing.

"You see, you might have a perfectly valid academic argument. Maybe it makes no rational sense at all for girls to have to wear tops—for there to be different dress codes for girls and boys. But the point is, you have to consider the consequences. Not only to yourself . . ."

She gazed at his hands. They were spread on his thighs—large, firm hands. "The consequences?" she whispered.

"Not only to you, but to me." He sighed. "Things like this scare people. It reminds them of all those protests and riots—you know. Tear gas. Helicopters. I told you about that in class."

Claudia moved away slightly. "But I didn't do anything so terrible! So many kids do worse things. You even told us—"

"You know as well as I there are a lot of buzzed-out kids on this campus. They might want to start something. Anything, just so it's anti-school. And something exciting. They don't care about issues."

"Some people have been writing letters to the school paper. They care."

"Look. Dr. Wallenburg has always given me a great deal of freedom with my teaching methods."

"You're the best teacher here!" she cried, amazed that she could say it, with him so close. "Everyone says so."

"I do my best." He smiled. "It isn't easy to get attention. Sometimes," he laughed, "you have to put on a whole bloody show. Like TV."

"A show?" It was a whisper.

"Oh, not that I don't mean it! I mean every word I say. It's just that—well, I've taught hundreds of students. Most of them don't take it so—so personally."

He stood up.

73

She, feeling foolish, did not know whether to stand or remain seated with him looking down at her. At last he gave her his hand, helped her up as if she were lovely and fragile, wearing a beautiful white gown.

"I'll tell you what I'll do," he said. "Let me talk to Mr. Milden for you. Maybe he'll reconsider about the social probation. It seems harsh to me. Meanwhile—just take it easy. Lie low. Don't get him upset at you." He smiled. "All right? Is that all right?"

Claudia nodded. Tears burned under her eyelids—she did not know why.

"Do you need a ride home?"

She shook her head. She had her bike.

"Well . . ." He gave her a smile and a wave. "Maybe next time."

They let her slink into the house and go to her room. They had probably discussed it. They called her once to dinner and allowed her to eat, did not make her speak or do the dishes. It seemed that nobody in this house would ever behave normally again.

Later Bennie phoned.

"Come on over and spend the night," she invited.

"Can't. I'm grounded."

"Bummer!"

"I'm a prisoner."

"Aren't we all."

"Ha-ha."

"Anything to cheer you up." Bennie chuckled. "See you at school."

"Maybe."

"What do you mean?"

"I could quit."

Bennie gasped. "And not graduate?"

"I could still get a diploma."

"They'll say you chickened out," said Bennie.

"Yes," said Claudia. "Look, I've gotta go."

Bennie paused. "I'm—I'm so sorry."

When the phone rang again, her mother came to her bedroom door. "For you," she said. "Again."

She would recognize that voice forever. David Beckett.

"So what happened to you?" he asked pleasantly, as if they had been conversing every night for the past four years.

"What did you think would happen?" She wanted to sound flippant and at the same time angry; she suceeded at neither.

"There's a rumor you were suspended."

"It's true."

"Wow. Hey, I'm sorry. I guess things got out of hand."

Her heart pounded terribly. She could hardly think. Oh, the clever, sarcastic remarks she might make if only she could think of them. She hated her fumbling stupidity, wished for the glibness of Glenda French, and Glenda's composure mixed with fiery temper—but nothing came to her. Nothing.

"Claudia? You still there?"

"Yes." *Still there, David, still waiting after four years. Idiot! If you knew how my heart was pounding.*

"So what happened Thursday morning?"

"You know about that?"

"I happened to talk to Denise Hunt."

"That bitch!"

David laughed, a short, astonished sound. "You're real tough, aren't you."

She did not answer. Then, "I was sent home again. Suspended people aren't allowed to be at school."

He chortled. "We should all be so lucky."

"You should have been suspended too."

"Oh, really? How do you figure that?"

"I got suspended for doing the same thing you guys were doing."

"Oh. I see. Sexual equality."

"That's right." Harder now, her heart pounded.

"What are you doing tonight?"

God—he was going to ask her out, ask her out! The dream, really coming true after all these years—what could she say? What would they talk about? It didn't matter, she could still remember how it felt when he kissed her, still remembered how it was being with him, the talk and the laughter and the excitement never ended.

"I'm grounded," she told him at last.

"Oh. I just wondered."

Later she wished with all her heart she hadn't asked him, but she did. "What are you doing tonight?"

"Oh, nothing much. Dillon and Margolis and I are just hanging around watching the Z channel. Just goofing off."

She thought she heard a faint snicker in the background.

"They're over there now?"

"Yeah. Something wrong?"

"No." She bit her teeth together, smiling into the telephone receiver as if her life depended on it, keeping herself from asking the obvious, "Why did you call?" knowing the answer, "Curiosity. Just goofing off."

When the phone rang again her mother hollered from the kitchen.

It had to be David Beckett, calling back. He would explain something, make things all right.

But it was Pete. The line from Santa Barbara was pocked with music, like whirling, windy sounds that made it seem as if the phone was bugged.

"What's doing?" he began.

"Not much. How are you?"

"Same old garbage." He sounded embarrassed. "How are your folks?"

"Fine."

He asked about everyone, stalling.

Pete seldom called long distance, except for a real

reason. Like when he'd invited her up for a fraternity rush dance last February. It seemed an eternity ago.

"Everyone is fine, Pete," she said, her pulse drumming. Why was she so scared? Pete loved her. During Christmas vacation he had told her again. Sure, he was dating other girls, but none like her. "You're my baby. Listen, you've got the most gorgeous body—let me have a picture of you in a bathing suit. I'll hang it in my room. The guys will . . ."

She asked. "What's new with you?"

"Well. I herd some really weird information."

"Really? What's it got to do with me?" Her legs felt weak, but another part of her was playing a role—wicked queen, Joan Crawford as the evil temptress in a movie.

"Uh—that you were—uh—involved in a thing at the swim meet this week."

"Oh, a thing? What kind of a thing?" Claudia's heart pounded now with that delicious surge of power fed by anger. She had never felt it so strongly before, and she was astounded.

"Are you trying to make this especially difficult?" he asked in an injured tone. "Because if you are, I think it's childish. I called because I heard some gossip, and I thought it was only fair to ask you first-hand."

"Well, I can't respond, can I," she said too sweetly, "until you tell me what it is."

"You took your top off," he said bluntly. "Everyone saw you—your—"

"My *what? What?*" *Say it!* she thundered inside herself, her whole body braced. *Say it!*

"That you went topless at the swim meet."

"Oh. So that's what they say at Santa Barbara."

"Is it true? Well, is it?"

He would be standing stiffly there by the phone, pulling in his lips the way he always did when he was mad. "Is it true?" he repeated.

There were a thousand things she wanted to say. To point

out that he was not her guardian. That it was none of his business. That what she wanted from her friends was support and understanding. That if he really loved her he would care how she felt now.

"I think you owe me . . ." Pete began.

The full tide of her anger rushed out. "Yes, Pete! Everyone at Menominee High Schol saw my boobs!" She was panting. "That's right. It's not so private anymore. You don't own me anymore—or any part of me!"

She slammed down the receiver so hard that the instrument made a little *ting!* Minutes later she heard the telephone ring again. But she had locked herself into the bathroom, turned on the water in the tub full force, so that her mother would have to tell him, "I'm sorry, Pete. Claudia's in the bathtub."

Saturday morning Vivian came over.

"You'll never guess what happened at the dance last night."

"You're right."

"We had a streaker."

"A—streaker? You mean . . . ?"

"Just before midnight. This guy comes up behind the band on the stage, wearing absolutely nothing but a Frankenstein mask."

"You're kidding."

"I swear. Everybody absolutely froze for a minute. Then they went wild. You can imagine. Everybody absolutely cracked up."

"David Beckett called me last night."

"Aren't you listening to me? This guy was *stark naked*."

"What's that got to do with me?"

"Claudia, you're being an absolute *wussy*. The guys all said it was Conrad Lorenz."

"So what?"

"Well, nobody did anything. The chaperones just—"

"How do they know it was Conrad Lorenz?"

"Oh, Claudia, don't be dumb. The guys know. They take P.E. together."

"So?"

"Good grief, maybe he's got a birthmark or a tattoo or— something distinctive about his—geez! I don't know. But Yale told me for sure it was Conrad. And a lot of the other guys said so, too."

"So, what if it really *was* Conrad?"

"Well, the chaperones just stood there and acted as if they were *spaced* that's what. Mr. MacIntosh and Miss Inaway just stood there and acted as if nothing had happened. They didn't even try to . . ."

"I see."

"Don't you care? Don't you understand?"

"Of course I understand!" Claudia cried. "They're going to ignore it, just because they weren't able to grab him. Or maybe his dad plays golf with somebody important. I understand that he'll never get suspended. He'll never get social probation. Vivian, *What am I supposed to do?*"

"I'm sorry," Vivian whispered. She sank down on Claudia's bed. "Maybe Marsha McClure was right. I saw her at the dance. In the restroom, after the streaker came, and everybody was going nuts. She was so furious about everything. About you."

"It's nice of her to . . ."

"She said all the girls should back you up. Start a real protest. Look, if two or three hundred girls went topless, they couldn't—"

"Oh, Vivian. They wouldn't. Anyhow, I don't want to go topless. I never did. That never was the point."

Vivian stood up to go, then turned, her face bitter. "By the way, Bennie's not supposed to associate with us."

"What are you talking about?"

"Her parents heard what happened at the dance and the swim meet. They questioned Bennie. You know how she can never tell a lie. Mrs. Murphy said we're a bad influence on Bennie."

"Bennie's seventeen years old! She's not a baby. When will they let her start living her own life?"

"Probably never. Did you know Mrs. Murphy is a member of that Women's League Committee on Education?"

"Mrs. Murphy? Why wouldn't Bennie have told me?"

"I don't think she ever knew," said Vivian thoughtfully. "My mother says that League could turn into a regular Gestapo. She says they're power hungry."

"What kind of power could they possibly want? Who cares about all this stuff?"

Vivian shrugged. "I don't know. Ask my mom. She says they're trying to take over this whole town. They've already got one man on the City Council, and my mom says they control one of the school board members. They're a scary bunch, according to my mom."

11

Looking back, it would take weeks to unravel it, to find the first cause of what the newspaper eventually called "complete polarization of the community."

At the time, I didn't even know what that meant. Now I know. It means people taking sides, getting locked into position, like fighters in their corners, all with too much to lose to back down.

I know it sounds crazy that such a little thing as one girl going topless at a swim meet can turn a whole community into a zoo—but that's how it is in towns like Menominee. I can think of lots of reasons. Maybe things had been too quiet for too long. People need a cause. At least that's what Mr. Xavier says.

Vivian's mom says it's all political—people will use any issue to get power. Like that Women's League. I don't know. It might sound weird, but I really didn't care about any of that. Not then. I had enough to worry about right at home.

My parents still weren't speaking to me. Oh, they talked to me, but you know what I mean. The AWFUL OFFENSE was always there in their eyes. They didn't trust me. Mom didn't ask me to do any errands. I didn't ask to use the car. I knew that any request would start a stream of accusations, and I couldn't bear it. I was too hurt.

It hurt that Bennie didn't call me, would hardly talk to me even in school. She's so pure, that Bennie. I suppose her parents made her swear she'd ignore me, making her feel incredibly guilty if she disobeyed. Poor Bennie. She looked miserable.

When my brother phoned, my mother told him what had happened. She thought I was outside, but I was in the dining room, so I heard. Apparently Scott didn't vote to have me boiled in oil. It sounded as if he was on my side. That really made my mother mad. For days she and my dad walked around with that expression on their faces, that what-have-we-done-to-deserve-kids-like-this look.

I phoned my brother on the sly.

"So, you're into that whole feminist thing," he said, laughing, eager.

"I don't know. I just took my damn top off. Now the sky is falling in."

"Cheer up," he said, so like his old self that I felt elated. "Some of the guys here think you're a hero. Or heroine."

I gasped. "Are you kidding? What do they know about it?"

"You know that item in *The Shore Times?* We'll, we've got a sister newspaper down here—those small papers have their own syndicate. I knew right away it was you."

"How could you?"

"I don't know. I just did. Vibes. Remember how when we were kids we always knew things about each other? Like when you got lost camping? And the day my tooth got knocked out?"

"Yes. I remember."

An unbelievable turn of events—my brother actually siding with me! It was wonderful—almost worth the price of my parents' anger.

Then Scott told me, "By the way, I'm applying to go to school in Europe next year."

"Will Dad let you?"

"I'll try to get a scholarship."

"Does he know?"

"Not yet. I . . ." He hesitated, then continued firmly, "I decided to transfer out of the business school. You remember that political science course I had last year, the one I told you about? Well, I've decided to take a poli sci major. To go into international relations. So, I figure it would be good for me to travel. See the world."

"That's wonderful, Scott."

"So, Dad's going to be—well, you know how he is."

Yes, I knew.

"I feel as if you've—I don't know. I was afraid to really go up against him. But now . . ." He hesitated. "Listen, Sis, take it easy. Keep your shirt on! Ha-ha!"

"Scott!"

"Yeah?"

"Let's keep the vibes going."

Isn't it incredible that doing one thing—one lousy little thing can change everybody's attitude about you?

I thought about that a lot. What it must be like to have committed a real crime. I mean, if you commit a robbery or a murder, suddenly everybody imagines you are a completely different person. Just because you did it. You no longer belong to the human race, almost. To the rest of the regulars. You know what I mean?

It was a little like that. Almost everybody I knew changed toward me in some way. In journalism, for instance, Miss Merriman suddenly started talking to me. I mean, really talking, telling me about her college days at Santa Cruz, her journalism class, her divorce.

She had two kids to support. Her husband had walked out

on her. Then, she couldn't even get credit. Not even one lousy credit card, and no loan from the bank to tide her over until she got back on her feet.

"It's a man's world," she told me grimly. "I—I'm proud of what you did. I understand it. Better than anyone, maybe."

My P.E. teacher looked at me differently, too. She was on my side. I could tell. I'd catch her watching me, and then she'd give me a grin, a wave, and I noticed how really young she is.

My Spanish teacher, Mrs. Paul, was a real creep. I'll never forget it.

We're supposed to be able to take make-up tests when we're absent. Even Mildew had told me I could make up the work I'd missed while I was suspended.

Monday afternoon I went in to take the make-up test during sixth period.

"You may sit in the back of the room and take the test," she said, handing me the paper, still watching her class with that hawk eye of hers.

I started to go to the back. I guess she focused on me.

"Wait a minute!" she yelled.

I turned back.

"Come here!"

I went to the desk, the test in my hand.

"Aren't you Claudia Warner?" she cried, so that everyone looked up to stare at me.

I nodded. I felt so humiliated—all those kids looking at me. They knew. Of course they did. Word gets around.

"You are not eligible to take that test!" Mrs. Paul snatched the test from my hand, and in a burst of venom, ripped it to bits.

"But—I'm supposed to be able to—I was absent."

"You were delinquent!" she shouted. "Delinquency is not a proper excuse. Delinquent students are not accorded make-up privileges."

I turned, blinded by tears of rage and embarrassment. She had no right!

As I walked out, I heard her screaming after me. ". . . disgusting, do you hear? Disgusting! I am putting an F in my book, do you hear? An F!"

I told Mr. Xavier about it. He really cared. I could tell. I waited for him in the parking lot again that day and told him what Mrs. Paul had done. I was still crying a little.

He handed me a tissue.

"Handkerchiefs," he said, "get too expensive in a place like this. Too many damsels in distress." He smiled.

"Do you do this often, then?" He was being so sweet.

"Oh, once or twice a day is all. It's hard to get through a whole day here without someone crying."

"Because people are so—so hateful!" I burst out. "That Mrs. Paul—the way she put me down!"

"*Hic semper tyrannis*," he said, smiling slightly. "That woman is a petty tyrant. Do you know Latin?"

"No. I don't want to, if it's the langauge of tyrants."

He laughed. I felt bright and clever.

He told me, "Listen, Claudia, I want to help you. I've been trying to see Mr. Milden. He keeps himself very busy. It might not hurt to let a few days go by, let things cool off."

"All right." I floundered over something to say to keep him there. Standing beside him talking seemed the only thing that could make me feel good.

"Well, I'd better be going," he said.

Dumbly I nodded, unable to look into his face, that face that I had memorized and that, in the night, now hovered in my mind just before I fell asleep.

It happened on Thursday. So oddly unrelated to anything involving me—yet in the end, the beginning of the turning point.

Let me go back. It might sound irrelevant—but wait. There's this kid called Lonnie Shrimpton, who's the ASB activities chairman. He plans things. Events. Well, The Shrimp had booked this terrific local rock group, The Planet Seven, to appear on our outdoor stage at noon on Thursday. It was a big event. See, everybody goes for The Planet Seven. They've got this mixture of rock and folk—well, you just have to hear them. Anyhow, The Shrimp got them for us. He has connections. His cousin produces records.

Later I found out what really happened. The Planet Seven actually did cancel just two days before the show. However, that's not what the rumor was. See, when The Planet Seven cancelled, The Shrimp just fell apart. He went home, sick. Some people had seen both him and Milden coming out of the office of the activities director, Miss Aguilar. Milden had been yelling about student conduct or something. So, naturally, when The Planet Seven cancelled, everyone assumed Milden had done it. There had been problems at the last two student activities; it was totally like Milden to do something like this. Everyone knew he hated music. Especially rock.

What happened next was total anarchy. At least that's what the papers called it. That's what the Women's League said in their statement—but I'm getting ahead of my story.

During second period, Miss Aguilar came on the PA system and announced what everybody already knew: The Planet Seven would not perform on Thursday.

I swear, you could feel the groan moving through the entire school.

In government class a note was dropped onto my desk. I hadn't seen the sender. "Some kids are planning a rally for Thursday. Interested?"

I looked up. From several aisles away Marsha McClure motioned, mouthing the words, "Meet me after class."

She cut her sixth period, and we talked. I couldn't believe

how involved people had already become, as if an entire underground network just lay waiting for action. During noon a bunch of people had gotten together.

"There's going to be a debate," Marsha told me excitedly. "They'll get Mr. Graham to sponsor it. You know how he goes for debates. A lot of kids are really bummed. It's one thing picking on individuals, but when Milden starts bullying the entire student body! We paid for that concert with our ASB funds."

"What's that got to do with me?" I asked.

"Everyone knows that Conrad Lorenz was the streaker. He didn't get punished. Everyone knows that this administration is unfair. Biased. Sexist."

"I see." I let out a long breath. "Marsha," I said, "I'm not a debater or an organizer. I'm not a—not what you think."

"Oh, yes, you are. I heard you in our government class. You were fabulous!" Her eyes shone. "Listen, a lot of people are really excited about this. It's our chance to change things. People are starting to get involved. Some guys approached me. Ross Mariannas andn Don Malvey and Tim Holmes."

"Malvey and Holmes! Marsha, those guys are—"

"I know what they are! It doesn't matter. They want to fight for us—don't you see? If enough kids petition the administration, they'll have to listen. Maybe they'll even get rid of Mildew. That would be the day! They'll remove your social probation. They'll revise those arbitrary rules—"

Marsha paused, gazing at me with those shining eyes. "You're a terrific speaker. Really. Like that woman lawyer, Glenda. You sound like her when you get fired up. So, maybe you could just say a few words . . ."

"No."

"No? Why not? You need support!"

87

"I need privacy!" I snapped. "I'm sorry, I just can't."

Marsha was undaunted. "I understand," she said softly, giving me a tender look. "You've been through so much. Don't worry. We'll take care of everything."

12

Things like this always start in an ordinary way. Later we would look back and say, "Oh, yes, I remember *exactly* how it was that day—the little electric gusts of wind— things crackled. People were jumpy, voices shrill. Everybody sort of jiggled with expectation."

Later you can say that. Then, it was just a usual day. Of course, I thought about what Marsha had said. Parts of it continually tangled in my dreams. But, waking, I went about my business.

Before school I had tried to see Milden. No dice. I heard his voice through the intercom. "Tell *Miss* Warner that I am making no appointments today. You may put her down for next week. *After* school."

Even the clerk eyed me coldly. Funny, how people copy the boss—actually, it's not funny.

At noon Vivian, Yale and I were wandering around the large grassy quad by the outdoor stage, where all the juniors and seniors hang out. Of course, there were reserved territories.

Cheerleaders and the other rah-rah's take the benches under the trees. Sosh's gather at the edge of the food lines, near the girls' lavatory. Athletes hang around that cemented area between the stage and the lawn, showing off. A few brains and wimps and band people claim the side wall of the band building, and the ASB officers, when they aren't running around smiling at people or looking terribly *busy*, congregate near the flagpole. Everybody else wanders in and out, trying to look casual.

I was thinking of taking off for the library. I don't like intruding. Vivian and Yale were being sweet, but I knew they'd rather be alone.

It started with a sound. Eerie and twanging, buzzing loud and louder, until we all froze, held our ears, cocked our heads. It was that electrical hum of a loudspeaker gone crazy. It filled your eyes, your head, that *twaannnggg*.

The alarming sound got everyone quiet. Into that stunned moment sprang our head cheerleader, Rob Wolcott, clutching the new cordless microphone and grinning like a gnome.

"Hey guys!" he screamed into the microphone. "Looks like we've got the makings of a little spirit rally. Whadda you say? Let's hear it for Menominee!"

"Menominee!" It was a tattered, cheerless response. Everyone knew Rob Wolcott had been waiting all month to get his hands on that new mike—what a show-off.

"Hey, that's great! Let's really hear it now," screamed Wolcott. "As you know, we were supposed to have a noon concert today."

This time the response was a roar. "Boo! Boo-whoo-oo!"

"Instead, we've got some records for you. But first, some of the gals from the pep squad are going to show us their new dance routine—aren't you gals?"

Whistles, leering and loud, followed the pep girls across the stage.

They gleamed and beamed, dancing to the yell:

Catch 'em
Can 'em
Hide 'em
Tan 'em
Run 'em down
Out of town
Let the word
Get around
MENOMINEE!

The girls wore short white gloves, mini-skirts and ruffled yellow panties. "All hands and asses," Yale said, and we laughed at them, feeling superior.

"Whatever turns you on," said Vivian, grinning.

I felt no sense of premonition, nothing but slight boredom. I was a senior. This was all so silly. It made me feel good to watch and not to care.

"Now, let's all come out to the Friday basketball game and give our support," shouted Rob Wolcott as the girls bounded off the stage. Rob leaped up and landed in a split. A groan and a cheer lapped through the audience—Rob would never know what a singular place he held with the students.

"And we all wanna show our appreciation to Lonny Shrimpton for his effort to—"

"Boo! Kill him! That little freak!" the kids jeered and yelled. Rob Wolcott seemed to think it was all in fun, all for spirit.

"So, just to show The Shrimp that we really love him," screamed Wolcott, "We'll dedicate this song to him."

It was a love song in a pulsating beat by The Planet Seven. People danced. Swayed. Dreamed.

"Pretty fantastic, eh?" hollered Wolcott when the song was over. "Now, guys, we've got another tune for you called 'Elephant Ears Hobo.'"

This song was not chosen by accident. Later, some of us

would realize this took somebody's precise planning, with everything ordered and for a purpose.

The song was loud, like the ocean. We drowned in it, in the sound, the meaning. People sat hugging their knees, braced against the deepness of it, the pain. We all knew about rejection. We all had suffered injustice. So what had begun as an ego trip for Rob Wolcott and the pep girls suddenly turned into something heavy—so heavy that when the song was over there was an eerie silence.

Into that silence stepped two boys, sober, wearing sport coats. You don't usually see boys in coats and ties at Menominee—unless there's something major happening.

But David Beckett and Greg Furrier stood there looking solemn and formal, positioned on either side of the microphone by the debate teacher, Mr. Graham.

You'd think, who in their right mind would stand there to hear a dumb debate? But something held the kids there. Maybe it was the way David and Greg stood, so straight and serious and expectant.

"Something happened here at Menominee High last week at the swim meet," said Greg. Each word was slow, distinct.

Oh, no. It couldn't be.

"It affects us all. One of our students, for reasons of her own, gave in to a certain idea, a form of expression . . ."

I wanted to die.

". . . resulted in unfair penalties by this administration. Regardless of our position on this one act, we have to face the real issue. A student's right to individual expression and, above all, equal rights and equal treatment of students, regardless of . . ."

Mr. Graham watched intently. This was what he loved. Debate. Issues. Students' rights versus school authority.

I stood, a statue painted onto carboard, feeling nothing, feeling everything. I glanced about. Vivian was not right there, but several feet away, jostled by the crowd. I thought people would heckle. Or leave. But they didn't. That song, "Elephant Ears Hobo," that song about injustice and abuse of power, had done its work. Nobody left. Nobody laughed.

On and on he spoke, Greg Furrier, eloquent in his convictions. ". . . we only ask that students be given equal treatment. Equal privileges and equal punishments. That rules consider individual rights, because once freedom is repressed, for whatever reason, none of us is safe from tyranny . . ."

But—but, if Greg Furrier was taking the *pro* side, that meant David Beckett was taking the *con*. But that was impossible. We had cared for each other once. Didn't that mean anything? It was one thing to get carried away in class, but to plot out a debate, to embarrass me beyond belief . . .

Furry continued. "Administrators should not react to pressure from outside groups. That results in unfair treatment. Too often this administration overreacts. It makes big issues out of simple problems. At other times, they totally ignore what's going on."

Cheers from the crowd. Furry was great. My skin prickled. I hadn't known he had it in him.

". . . we have freedom of the press. But when the administration tries to tell us what to print . . ."

Obviously, Mr. Milden was trying to get Greg, as assistant editor, to slant the news. I could understand Greg's stance in the debate. But David? People knew we used to go together. Somehow, even as I watched David standing there waiting for his turn, I already knew it was going to become personal and hateful.

It did. David was all fired up. It was as though he had prepared for and lived for this moment—to hold the crowd in his hands, to thrill to their cheers, to blaze out at them and at me, as if he had been so personally threatened and attacked that he had to smash everything in his way. His sentences were short, powerful bursts of power, like gunshots—after each came a hail of applause.

"No one person can be allowed to decide the standard for all!

"Are we going to let all the loudest, all the craziest people run this school?

"It's simple. If you break the rules, you deserve to get punished. Any other code takes us back to the jungle!"

What happened next could never be again. The timing was superb. At the word "jungle" a roar burst out from somewhere. Heads turned. Shouts of astonishment and delight burst through the crowd as laughter replaced anxiety.

I whirled around, saw David Beckett laughing and making comic gestures. In an instant he had changed from crusader to clown. I was appalled. And then it hit me with all the force of a brick. Later I would think it through—at that moment the knowledge was not clearly defined, only felt. David Beckett would go around hurting people all his life, never caring. In fact, he'd probably never know the difference. Because that was the way he was. He had to be the winner and the boss, no matter what—he had to come out on top. I shuddered for all the girls who would yet love him.

Later, later I pondered this. Now everyone turned. It was too good to miss. Around the flagpole danced the two crazies, Joanie Truitt and Fay Allison, screaming like monkeys and dressed alike in bright red leotards. With them, like pipers of old, came a boy playing the trumpet, another the saxophone and a third with a tuba. Over and over they played the same bellowing tune while Joanie and Fay leaped and screamed and danced. Joanie wore a huge sandwich sign that said MILDEW SUCKS. Fay had made the two different signs into a single banner: COVER THE WORLD WITH TOPLESS TONIGHT.

People broke away to follow, winding in and out like the paper dragon in a Chinese New Year parade. No call for order from Wolcott or Beckett, Greg Furrier or Mr. Graham could change the course of this rally, which took on a life and purpose of its own.

Events followed so swiftly that they flashed like slides onto a screen. In a twinkling the flag was lowered down the pole. Hoisted up under it was a shirt, hung by its sleeve. It was my old blue workshirt. Painted on the back in white block letters was the word FREEDOM.

What happened next was the shock of being seized and lifted up, up onto the shoulders of two boys, with several others jostling close. Strong arms held me, laughter and shouting filled my senses as they marched with me into the whirling crowd. I saw it all from above, caught up in the madness, bobbing above it like a giant balloon.

I heard echo after echo of my name. I saw faces suddenly made intimate by a sense of joy—Marsha McClure, Connie Philips, Don Malvey, Tim Holmes, Ross Mariannas—guys I'd never talked to, guys who always seemed so strange and distant. They were shouting my name! I caught flashes of people and buildings, saw a glimpse of Mr. Xavier's face and gloried in his presence. A beam of sun hit the tuba. Notes vibrated and bounced against buildings and bodies. It was insane. My throat was raw from screaming. My face was wet. I was being born atop an ocean wave that surged toward shore.

When the fire alarm went off, everyone screamed.

The first fire engine rolled through the gate, siren blaring, horn blasting. Then came the paramedics and the squad car. The sound of breaking glass brought me back.

Afterward, I cut my government class. I didn't want Mr. Xavier to see me. I spent about fifteen minutes in the girl's lavatory holding wet paper towels to my face, trying to fix my hair.

Outside, everyone had dispersed. The last fire engine rolled away. As I made my way out the gate, I heard someone call my name.

"Miss Warner!" he said.

I turned and saw a tall thin young man wearing a raincoat that looked several sizes too large for him. Even his shoes were too big. They were brown loafers, cracked from rain and tipped up at the toes. Something about him made me want to laugh, to meet his hand as he extended his.

"Stan Bliss," he said. "From *The Shore Times*."

I recoiled, said bitterly, "Not interested."

"I'd just like to talk to you," he said. "I thought I'd give you an opportunity to tell your side of the story."

"I know that trick," I retorted. "I'm in journalism, too."

"I covered the swim meet last week," he said.

"No comment." I felt my face flush.

"I've talked to your mother, and—"

My heart pounded with outrage. "I don't believe you! My mother doesn't talk to reporters."

"She did this time. So, I thought maybe you'd want to tell me your side."

"I *have* no side." I gritted my teeth. "I'm all front, don't you know? I'm the *Playboy* centerfold for June."

"I realize you're angry at—at the situation," he said calmly. "I just happen to be getting the fall-out."

Disgusted, I turned away.

He rushed after me, stuck his card inside my book. "In case you change your mind," he said.

"I won't."

"Call me if you do. By the way, I used to play basketball with your brother, Scott."

Liar! I thought, furious, then taunted him, "And I suppose you just happened to be driving by when you heard the fire trucks?"

"Exactly right," he said. "I just keep getting lucky at this school."

I never had a chance to ask my mother about this Stan Bliss character, because that night my brother phoned. He told them about his plan to spend a year studying in Europe. After that, they went on for hours. For a change, at least, they were off my case.

13

During second period a messenger came to the class. Mrs. Paul read the note, her mouth puckered in disgust. "Claudia Warner! Principal's office. Now."

In all her years of school, Claudia had never been summoned to the principal's office until now. People had never stared at her or talked about her.

It was a new feeling, walking through the halls, knowing that people nudged each other when she passed, spoke her name. Some called to her with open admiration: "Hey, Claudia! How's it goin'?"

Just those few words, nothing more—amazing, what a difference it made to be known. To be not only part of something, but at the center. The entire campus was alive with the aftermath of the rally. People like Marsha McClure and Connie Philips talked of nothing else, buzzed around busily, looking important. This was something they would all remember; it would be woven into the fabric of their school life, becoming legend. And Claudia was in it. She had made herself count for something after all.

The messenger was a freshman girl. Now Claudia understood how it was that kids in trouble often assumed that swaggering air of total nonchalance. She felt it in her own posture as she followed the girl, in the swing of her hair and the slight smile on her face.

"Who wants me?" she asked the girl when they were out in the hall. "Old Mildew?"

The girl giggled. "I think Dr. Wallenburg."

"Oh. Wally." Claudia walked on beside the girl, remembering yesterday's feeling of being borne high, high on the shoulders of her classmates, an exaltation so strong that it moved her beyond laughter, to tears.

Outside the office the clerk made her wait. "Have a seat, please."

"Thanks," said Claudia. "I'll stand."

"Suit yourself." The clerk gave her a terrible look.

Soon she was called inside.

Dr. Wallenburg looked pristine in a pale blue knitted suit. Not a single hair was out of place. Her skin was smooth, her lips carefully outlined.

Now, sitting opposite the principal, Claudia felt again altered. Like a child called in for naughtiness, she bit her lip, regretted the condition of her shoes, her fingernails, which were short and stubby. In the presence of Dr. Wallenburg, she felt awkward, embarrassed by yesterday.

Dr. Wallenburg's tone was moderate, impartial. "You and I have some problems to work out, Claudia."

Claudia nodded.

"I didn't witness the rally yesterday. I was having lunch in the teacher's cafeteria. Then the fire alarm went off. Of course, that did get my attention." She smiled slightly, a delicate attempt at humor.

"It puzzles me," the principal continued, "when a girl like you changes so suddenly. Perhaps there are external influences. Or could it be the excitement of your senior year?"

Claudia sighed. "I don't know."

"You've always been cooperative. No U's on your

record. Good grades. Participation in the music program . . ."

Sentences seemed to float before Claudia's eyes. "Does being good mean you never say anything when things are unfair?"

Dr. Wallenburg's spine stiffened. She leaned toward Claudia, her hands folded tightly on the desk. "Claudia, you know that in any society, any institution, there must be rules. We cannot allow rules to be flaunted. The result is anarchy. You know that."

"Sometimes a person has to break a rule," Claudia said, "to test it."

"Ah, yes." Dr. Wallenburg sighed. "That used to be the fashion. I do remember." She smiled slightly. "When my mother was a student, she tells me they used to crowd as many kids as they could into a phone booth. Before that, youngsters swallowed live goldfish and sat on top of flag poles—all to prove something. Do you get my point?" She was smiling as if they were friends.

"This is different. Those were just silly pranks."

"Well." Dr. Wallenburg smoothed her hand over her desk. "It's all a matter of perspective. Someday you will see this quite differently. It would be a shame to escalate a minor mistake into a total disaster. I'm sure you get my point."

Claudia could think of no reply. All her life, it seemed, she had been ruled by other people's words. It occurred to her that a single act is better than a thousand words.

"I think it might be a good idea for you to see Mrs. Thatcher, Claudia. Talk to her. Get to the root of your problem. It's no disgrace to—"

"You want me to see the psychologist?"

"Sometimes tensions build up and cause us to behave in ways—"

"I don't want to see the psychologist."

"I see." Like a person whose best offer had been refused,

Dr. Wallenburg withdrew, leaning back, her hands clasped at the edge of her desk. "Then you are quite comfortable with your behavior."

"I'm not comfortable," said Claudia. Inside, she was burning as with fever.

"You know," said Dr. Wallenburg, smiling again, "it happens sometimes that young people get carried away. Or influenced by others. I understand that Mr. Xavier—"

"He had nothing to—"

"Oh, I know all the girls are quite taken with Mr. Xavier." The principal chuckled. "And he is a very—ah—dynamic teacher. He has really set a lot of girls a-flutter here."

"Mr. Xavier had nothing to do with it!" Claudia cried. She knew she sounded defiant and rude, that her gestures were harsh and her eyes bright with anger. She didn't care.

"Let me tell you how it looks from my side of the desk," said Dr. Wallenburg sternly. She strained toward Claudia, each point punctuated by a nod of her head.

"I have had dozens of telephone calls from angry parents. They want to know what is going on here. I don't blame them.

"This morning I had a telephone call from the American Civil Liberties Union. Their attorney is investigating charges that I am censoring the school newspaper.

"I have received a petition signed by two hundred students asking for removal of your social probation."

Claudia's eyes widened. "A petition! I never . . ."

"Meanwhile, *The Shore Times* is running articles continually, fomenting dissention in the community. Your mother is making statements to the press about how we are unfair to—"

"My mother! Dr. Wallenburg, wait. What do you mean? My mother hasn't given any statements. She wouldn't."

"She has, Claudia! It's right here in *The Shore Times*, this morning's edition." Dr. Wallenburg snatched up the paper,

101

slammed it down onto the desk in a swift, brief outburst. "But I'm not finished! Yesterday's fire alarm will cost the city fifteen hundred dollars. Part of that comes out of our school budget. In case you don't know, there was even a spot about the false alarm on the evening television news. Mr. Spengler, president of the school board, made sure to inform me about that this morning."

The principal gasped, coughed, then continued more vehement than before. "Now the television station, I understand, is considering doing a documentary called 'Schools in Transition.' They are looking at Menominee High. They are planning, if I know anything at all about the media, to paint a picture of total chaos. Disregard for authority. Vandalism and riot. A crisis in education, Claudia! The sort of thing you were at the center of yesterday! And you sit there acting as if none of this has occurred!"

Claudia sat stunned, amazed. Like a house of cards, it was all falling down around her. Why? How could the world be so very fragile? Why couldn't the grown-ups in charge keep it together?

Dr. Wallenburg gave a great sigh. She pushed back her chair as if everything had been settled. "Now," she said, "where do we go from here? I will tell you.

"First," she said, "the broken windows have to be paid for. We can work that out with your parents."

"My parents?" Claudia felt the blood drain from her face.

"Secondly, you should know that at this moment I am under great pressure to have you expelled—not only from the Women's League Committee on Education, but by members of our own school board."

Expelled!

Suddenly Claudia began to tremble, and she burst out, "Why me? I never broke those windows. I didn't start that rally. They asked me to—I refused. All I did was be there,

102

like everyone else. How can I help it those guys lifted me up? What I did at the swim meet—I've already been punished for that! Suddenly I take the blame for everything. Conrad Lorenz ran stark naked through the dance. Everyone knows it. What happened to him? Nothing! Nothing! What about the boys smoking pot in the east bathroom? All the teachers pretend they don't know! And the kids who ditch school and go down to the cliffs to drink beer—and last year at the senior prom, Monty Haddigan and some other guys were taking cocaine. *Cocaine!* Why didn't they get expelled or even suspended? Why me?"

In the ensuing silence the wall clock made a little jumping sound. Dr. Wallenburg sat frozen in the attitude of listening, her brow furrowed and hands clasped. Her expression said it all—see? There is something terribly wrong with you, child. You are hysterical. You need help.

At last Dr. Wallenburg spoke. "Well," she said briskly, "that was that. Now we must look to the future. From now on, Claudia, it will be best for you to keep off the schoolyard during noon time. Come in here to my office. I will find something for you to do."

She continued, her tone almost pleasant. "I see you do not have a sixth period. I want you to go home immediately after your last class. As for the broken windows, I do want to be fair. I see your point. Perhaps we can arrange something to prevent your actually having to pay for them, since you were not actually involved in the breakage. But I am going to insist that you come to school for the next three Saturday mornings and join the clean-up patrol."

Claudia felt sick. Clean-up patrol was for the worst kids, delinquents always in trouble with the cops, kids from the Continuation School. They walked around with big gunny sacks picking up junk. Or they were given hoes and told to weed the vast hillsides behind the school.

"It isn't fair," Claudia whispered.

"Let me tell you, Claudia. I'm saving your neck. What I

am asking is more than fair. Do you realize how an expulsion would look on your record?"

Claudia shook her head. Unbidden tears rolled down her cheeks. She stiffened against the sobs, held them in.

"Don't jeopardize your whole future over this—this nonsense," said the principal. She picked up Claudia's folder. "You are a bright girl. A B-plus student. Let me give you some advice. This can still be smoothed out and forgotten. If not—universities can cancel acceptances. Nobody wants a troublemaker on campus."

Claudia, despite her tears, recognized the thinly veiled threat. Someone—someone could say something to the university entrance committee; it was possible. She knew that now.

Dr. Wallenburg stood up. She smiled. "Remember. No more talking to the press. No agitating. Come in here at noontime. And you owe me three Saturday mornings."

Claudia stood up. She did not speak or move.

"You keep your part of the bargain," said Dr. Wallenburg, "and I'll discuss the situation with Mr. Milden. We could compromise and allow you to participate in the last week of senior activities. Then you could participate in the graduation exercises. And you could play in the senior talent show."

Dr. Wallenburg gave a final nod. "We would like you to graduate from Menominee High with good feelings."

Outside, Claudia gagged.

She ran to the far end of the administration building to the bushes, where she lost her breakfast.

14

In the journalism room Claudia found a copy of the morning *Shore Times*.

Even when she saw the article printed there, and her mother's photograph smiling faintly at her through the newsprint, it seemed unreal. Her mother talking to the press? And not even mentioning it? Well, last night she and Dad had had the blow-up about Scott changing his major and going to Europe. Still, Claudia could not imagine her mother giving a statement, any statement, without checking with Dad first.

The caption under the photograph read: Coed Mother Criticizes Handling of Topless Incident.

Lines of type seemed to leap out from the page, defying continuity. ". . . don't agree with what she did . . . my daughter is a fine musician . . . should be allowed to play for the senior show."

The rest of the article seemed like a queer patchwork of her life, pieces taken out of context to create a person mildly resembling Claudia Warner. But the words were as far from the reality as the photograph of her mother was from the woman she knew.

She read the words over and over again ". . . the attractive coed . . . journalism student . . . classmates are divided on . . . some accuse the administration of censorship . . . the pretty blonde senior is an accomplished musician . . . mother involved in her own career."

Miss Merriman came to sit down beside her.

"What do you think of the article?"

"I feel robbed. Are they allowed to print things without checking with me?"

"You know they are," said Miss Merriman. Her manner was easy, her tone gentle. "I thought the reporter would have interviewed you."

"He tried. I wouldn't talk to him. Are they allowed to use people's names like that?"

"The law protects juveniles accused of crimes from being publicly named. What you did was no crime. It only says things about you that are true—you did win the music prize. You are blonde and a senior . . ."

"Why do they always call people attractive? Why mention the color of their hair?"

Miss Merriman smiled. "I'm glad you noticed that. They don't always. Just for females."

"I feel—robbed," Claudia said again. "My right of privacy—what about that?"

"When a person does something newsworthy in public, they can't later claim the right of privacy." She stood up. "But you know all this, Claudia. You've been in my journalism class for two years. It just feels different when you're the target, doesn't it."

Once again Claudia scanned the article. "Mrs. Warner, one of the area's three top sales people for LovLee Cosmetics, indicated displeasure with the administration's handling of her daughter's situation."

"Your mother sounds like a nice lady," said Miss Merriman. "A strong person. You must take after her."

* * *

She was about to leave with the others when Mr. Xavier called her back.

He seemed strained, agitated. She could see the glaze of perspiration on his forehead and upper lip.

He closed the back door, motioned for her to come and sit down beside him. He leaned back, stretched out his legs. She did not want to look at his body, did not know where to focus her eyes.

"Claudia," he said softly, and she watched the movements of his throat as he spoke. "Claudia, I find myself in a very awkward position."

What was he saying?"

"I had a talk with Dr. Wallenburg today at noon. She called me in."

You, too? Is she persecuting you, too?

"I understand you were in to see her earlier."

"Yes."

She could tell, he hated Dr. Wallenburg. He had certainly defied her. Told her to lay off Claudia, his student, only acting from her ideals and convictions—*he had told her! You can take your job and shove it!* just like that song.

"You see, Dr. Wallenburg is in a very difficult position. She is being pressured from all sides."

Dully Claudia nodded. *So am I.*

"Look, nobody is trying to minimize the extent of your—your struggle. I mean, I know very well that your motive was commendable. You were thinking of equality. You were doing your utmost to make a—a statement."

No. I did it on impulse. But now—everyone has changed it.

"But things have gotten out of control. Surely you don't want to see this student body divided. To be responsible for chaos. There is a time," he said, gazing at her, "when it is noble to retreat."

He leaned toward her. She could not avoid his eyes or the

107

heavy thudding of her heartbeat. There was so much she wanted to explain to him.

"Dr. Wallenburg is a person of—of moderation. I understand she has offered you a way out. A fair compromise. Now, all you have to do is—"

"She wants to lock me up," Claudia said, straining from some depth of her being. "She wants me to come work for her every noon, do clean-up on Saturdays. Is that fair? She blames me for the things I never did, punishes me just to show the Women's League Committee that she's tough! Is that fair? Is that—"

"Claudia, for God's sake! My job is on the line here. Do you understand? My *ass* is on the *line*. What is fair is—"

The door burst open. "Hi! I thought you asked me to meet you . . ."

Glenda French moved in, a flash of energy.

"Oh, I'm sorry. Didn't mean to interrupt. Hello, Claudia. I heard about that trouble. Are they giving you a tough time?"

"Glenda, we'll be late," said Mr. Xavier, leading her to the door.

"Philip, wait a minute."

"She'll be fine, Glenda. We've got it all worked out."

"It's OK," said Claudia.

"I heard about that Women's League Committee," Glenda said. "They love to sink their teeth into something like this. They're book burners!"

"Now, Glenda, they never actually burned anything." Mr. Xavier said. "Come on. I thought you wanted to go."

"Those women aren't elected or appointed by anybody in office!" Glenda cried. "They're just a bunch of self-appointed, self-righteous old busybodies!"

"So what?" cried Mr. Xavier. He snapped out the lights, pushed open the door. "People like that are best ignored—just a few harmless old ladies."

"I don't think they're so harmless," snapped Glenda. She turned to Claudia. "Do you?"

"Glenda!" Mr. Xavier shouted. "This is not your business. Will you please stay out of it? Will you please stay away from my school?"

Glenda reached into her bag, drew out a card and gave it to Claudia. "Call me," she said, "if you want to talk. Anytime."

Claudia watched them leave. They seemed tense, as if they might still quarrel. Then he said something. They both laughed. He took her arm, and Claudia saw that Glenda's step matched his exactly.

For the first hour at home her father had said nothing. He thrust his briefcase down by the coatrack, went into the kitchen where he filled a glass with ice and added a measure of whiskey. He drank it down fast, like the gunmen in Westerns, his eyes steely and forward facing.

"What is it, Walt?" Her mother came from the sink, drying her hands, smiling tentatively. "Did you have a bad day?"

Claudia, out in the laundry room, froze.

He said nothing. She heard his retreating footsteps, muffled on the living room carpet, and her mother's refrain. "What is it, Walt? Won't you tell me? What's the matter?"

Silence, at last, made its own sound in the house, lifted the ordinary clatter of silverware and dishes to a harsh crescendo. They ate. Nobody spoke. Once Claudia's mother motioned for her to pass the bread, then said thank you.

Afterward, Claudia went to her room. The flute lay in its case untouched these last two weeks. Now she brought it out, set Mrs. Seymour's composition onto the music stand and began to play.

It was a beautiful, lyrical, exciting piece. It ought to be performed. All she had to do was relent. Compromise. Allow Dr. Wallenburg the benefit of the doubt—she meant well. Actually, she was not a bad person. The piece ought to be performed, for Mrs. Seymour's sake.

Play! Play! In her mind Claudia heard the music teacher's beating hands, saw her snapping eyes, felt her own breath and heartbeat and spirit blending with the music—play!

But at what price?

The notes leaped and curved and curled, rose in grand arpeggios, slid down again, then higher and higher into a swift staccato burst of joyous birdsong—swinging down now to an even, a gentle, a final resolution, yet with emotion lingering there.

The last note held, like a muted color settling over her things, the way sunset brings bluish shadows into a room.

Then, the cry. "Why are you being so c-c-cruel to me? Don't you think I have the right to . . ."

Claudia crept out into the small hallway. She and Scott used to do this together, adventuring, "Let's go listen in the hall!"

"You can't imagine how it feels," her father said grimly, "to have people calling you. People who used to respect you, to tell you your wife's picture is in the newspaper. Then to have to pretend you knew about it. Because otherwise you look like a complete idiot!

"You can't imagine, Doreen. Not to speak of what this will mean to my reputation in town. And you know very well that in a business like mine reputation is everything."

"I was only being pleasant. He didn't trick me."

"He didn't trick you, Doreen? You mean you just happened to discover this nice young man as you were coming out of the supermarket, and you just happened to tell him—"

"Walt, you make it sound so childish and stupid! I only . . ."

"When will you stop being 'pleasant' to people, Doreen? If it hurts your husband, your family, your livelihood? When are you going to start using your head?"

"But it won't hurt us, Walt. Really. I was going to tell you. Dottie Freeman called and said she saw the article. She said it was good publicity for me. She said I'll get many more calls, and that people will think it was great that I stuck up for my daughter."

"Dottie Freeman," he shouted, "is an idiot! She's got the brains of a snail."

"Mrs. Norford called me too."

"Mrs. Norford? Called you?"

"Why, yes."

"Good God, what did she say?"

"She said it was a nice picture of me. She said it reminded her that she'd been wanting to call me."

"Mrs. Norford has been wanting to call you, Doreen? Didn't you find that just a little bit peculiar? This woman you've only met once before?"

"No, no. I saw her at the Christmas boutique and again at that Town Hall reception we went to."

"So you met her twice! So what? She's the wife of a school board member. Doesn't that faze you?"

"She wants me to give a demonstration for her church group in a month or so. She'd been *meaning* to call me."

"Oh, Doreen! How can you be so naive?"

In the hall Claudia shivered. She waited through the protracted silence, imagining her mother recoiling into tears of helplessness and defeat.

But it was not so. In the next moment her mother's voice rang as never before. "You would take even this away from me! How dare you? You say you love me. You keep me like—like a child, a pet, a prisoner!"

"What are you talking about? What are you talking about?"

"*You listen!* Ever since I got my job you've been jealous."

"Doreen, don't be ridiculous."

"You never wanted me to do well, to have something all

111

my own. Oh, you *said* it, but every time I tried to do something, you were there blocking me, making me feel like a—*incompetent*."

"What are you talking about? I was the one who encouraged you. I told you to buy yourself those new clothes so you'd look professional. I referred you to those gals at Mayflower Center. I've done everything for you!"

"Then maybe that's the trouble."

The finality in her mother's tone astounded Claudia. She crept into the kitchen. It was dark. She opened the refrigerator, needing its light, afraid to switch on the big light overhead. Automatically she took an apple, stood rubbing it against her sleeve.

"And I think you are making a big mistake, Walter." Her mother's voice was flat, final, like the *coda* in a piece of music. "You haven't talked to that child for nearly two weeks."

"I have nothing to say to her."

"She's your daughter."

"I know! And it makes me sick!"

She tried to phone Scott. His roommate said he was out. Claudia lay on her bed watching the faint moonlight through the curtains make patterns on the wall.

Vivian was out with Yale. Bennie was incommunicado. *Where have all the people gone?*

She reached down, brought Chaucer up from the braided rug beside her bed. She placed him on her chest, so that she could feel his sleek fur against her chin. His bronze-green eyes glowed like jewels.

"Cats are perfect," she whispered. "No jealously. No greed. They're never too busy. Never get mad for no reason. Never turn on you."

Chaucer switched his tail, began kneading with his paws. The nail tips were sharp; she held the paws in her hand, cushioning the points. Still the cat kneaded and purred. He loved her. Unconditionally. That, she thought, was the great thing about cats. They do not trade love for good behavior or pride or pleasure. They are independent, but generous.

"Few others," she whispered, "can make that claim."

David Beckett. He could trade emotions the way a lizard sheds an old skin. Pete. What he needed of her had nothing to do with *her*. Bennie—poor Bennie, so utterly dominated. Her own father. And mother. And now, Mr. Xavier.

She had not allowed herself to think of him. Not yet. Now as she lay with the cat, she realized that she would not cry. She would end it here, though it would never be over completely. Always, she would remember him, the way he was in class, so passionately *noble*—and then she would hear him say, "I've got my ass on the line!"

He, who had caused an entire class to rise and applaud, who never had an empty seat in his classroom, who talked with his disciples under the trees, until the talk became an object in itself, a tangible reality, something to keep forever.

He had shoued, "My *ass* is on the line!"

Were she different, had she been wiser and quicker, she would have turned to him and retorted, "Of course it is. That's just the point, *Philip!* Don't you see?"

Strange, how she had rushed to the library for him. Taken a front seat—for him. Waited for hours to pry a few extra words from him. Then to hear him tell her that he had taught hundreds of students and none of them took it so *personally*.

Chaucer leaped off. He moved stealthily toward the wall, then pounced at the moon shadow. Claudia sighed. Maybe that was the trouble. Taking things personally. Of course, that was what made some people different from animals. Even from this beloved cat.

15

When Claudia woke up on Saturday morning she knew her father was gone. Somehow she could tell.

Mom had the stereo on. Yes, that was it. When he was home her father would complain, "Would you please turn that thing off, Doreen?"

Claudia got up, pulled on her robe. She'd had it since she was twelve. That was the great thing about robes—you could grow and change, but the old robe lasted, became more comfortable.

Her mother was polishing her nails at the kitchen table. Carefully she dipped in the brush, let it rest on the rim for a moment, brought it to the nail with precise, even strokes, just three to each nail. Claudia had seen it a thousand times, always fascinated.

"Your nails look nice," she said.

"Thanks, dear. Oh, don't jiggle the table when you sit down."

"I won't."

"You want to fix yourself some eggs?"

"I will later."

"Your father went fishing."

"I know."

"How?"

"The stereo."

"Oh."

It hung between them, their common knowledge of him. His demands. The awareness that it was different—better— when he was gone. Better between the two of them.

Her mother sighed, capped the polish, sat with her hands spread flat on the table. "You know, he was really a nice young man. Not pushy or anything."

The reporter, Claudia realized.

"That's why I talked to him. I was just coming home from the market. He was pleasant. Not tricky or mean."

Claudia glanced at her mother's face, saw the anger.

"I have that right!" she exclaimed.

"Of course you do, Mom. You can talk to anybody you want."

"I've had four phone calls about it." Her mother blinked rapidly, took a deep breath. "Three on Friday. One this morning. I never realized people save that paper and read it the next day. Shirlee Harvey read it. She said it was great the way I got involved. Involved, she said. Shirlee is always involved in something. I mean, she's so active."

"Well, so are you, Mom. You have a job."

"Yes, that's so! Shirlee said it should have been in the paper last year when I won third place in the sales contest. She said things like that make a difference. That reporter asked me about my job. I didn't tell him to put in that part about winning the contest, but when he asked me about my work, I remembered it. It seemed important."

"You should be proud of that," said Claudia.

"And I am! But your father seems to think it's some kind of a joke. Like when they gave me the prize—the travel case—and he said, 'Oh, of course it would be *pink*. Now I suppose you'll want to buy all matching pink luggage!' I don't like it when he puts down my job. Do you think he has

115

any idea what it's really like? All he sees are those pink boxes."

Her mother sat imprisoned at the table with her hands out flat. Claudia could see the anger in her eyes, in the quickness of her breath.

"I have to get up early every day. Get out early. I never sleep in. It's not easy to get yourself all made up. I mean, I've got to look the part. Nails done. Hair perfect. Makeup the best I can do—everything coordinated."

Her mother's tone, sharp and passionate, held Claudia bound. Her mother, flawless even now in her crisp, flowered model's coat and immaculate yellow espadrilles— her mother looked very old and somehow also very young.

"It's hard to be coordinated all the time." It was a muffled whisper, the agony showing through.

Claudia nodded. Never had they cried together. Nor would they now.

Claudia got up, went to the counter, took a tissue from the box. Wordlessly she laid the tissue onto the table. Then, seeing her mother's hands spread out flat, she took the tissue, carefully folded it and reached out to dab the slight spill of tears from her mother's cheeks.

"There," she said. She made her voice bright. "I love you, Mom!"

Her mother smiled crookedly. "I feel like a baby."

Claudia asked, "You want some eggs?"

"Well . . ."

"Only seventy-five calories apiece! Loads of protein!"

"All right. Why not?"

Swiftly Claudia broke the eggs into a bowl, taking care to notice every detail, the yolk, the white, the shining glass bowl. It all seemed very important, the sort of detail she would remember in later years—whipping up the eggs, melting the butter, feeling the overpowering urge to sing out loud and also to cry.

"Eggs a la Claudia," she said with a smile and a flourish.

"Thank you, darling." Her mother's voice was soft again, her expression subdued.

Claudia walked to Vivian's house. She rang until at last Vivian appeared from the backyard, her hands, shoes and jeans splotched with mud.

"Hi. I'm planting."

"Uh-oh." Whenever Vivian got upset, she dug in the garden. Each year Vivian's mom hoped her daughter would get good and mad in the spring; it assured them a fine crop of summer vegetables.

"What's wrong?"

"Yale. We've split."

"Viv! How could you? You've been going together so long. You're so in love!"

"I realized we don't actually have anything in common. We're completely different."

"Viv, that isn't true. The two of you are great together."

"It's over." Vivian sat down, wiped her hands on the grass.

Claudia settled beside her. "Want to tell me about it?"

"Nothing to tell. He just acted like a real jerk. He gets so completely immature sometimes, acting like some macho killer in the movies—it makes me sick."

"It's because of me," Claudia stated. "Isn't it?"

Vivian looked up, surprised. "Oh, good grief. It—it isn't *really*. I never knew he could be so—chauvinistic. I mean, he's really a pig, you know." Vivian bit her lip, about to cry.

"What happened?"

"Did you know Pete was here for the weekend?"

"No."

"He's here for some dumb fraternity thing. Anyhow, Yale and I were over at Corry's last night with a bunch of kids. Pete was there."

"You know why I went with Pete?" Claudia suddenly said.

117

Vivian shook her head slowly. "I thought you loved him."

"I *wanted* to. I wanted to be going with somebody, especially a senior. Is that terrible? And dumb?"

"Look, Pete is a nice guy. It didn't have to be permanent."

"That's the thing. He's '*such a nice guy.*' One of the few boys I ever went out with who didn't keep hassling me about going to bed. So I—felt secure with Pete. You know?"

"Yeah. I know."

"Except, that's not love. It's kind of using somebody. And I guess he was using me, too."

"Yup." Vivian nodded vigorously. "I think he let the other guys *think* you were . . ."

They sat, brooding, sorrowing. "I think so too," Claudia said at last.

"Good riddance!" cried out Vivian. She quickly brushed her cheek with her hand. "Good riddance to all of them! Men!"

"What did Yale do?"

"He and Pete were talking. Loud. Acting so spaced—you know how they can get at a party, talking about . . ."

"The swim meet?"

"All that stuff. And Yale goes, well, if any dame ever did that to me, I'd drop her like a hot potato. So I said, what do you mean, did that to *you?* So he says, well, if I was going with a girl and she showed her tits to everybody, we'd be through. It's damn embarrassing to have your old lady go around showing herself—I mean, it gives a guy a really weird reputation."

"Yale said that?"

Vivian nodded.

"Then what?"

"I called him a bunch of awful names, which I don't feel like repeating. It was awful."

They sat plucking out blades of grass, nibbling the tender ends. "Why are guys like that?"

"They think they own you."

"Sometimes they almost do."

"Not me," Vivian said grimly. "Never again." Fiercely she pulled at a cluster of crab grass, brought forth a long root.

"Are you going to keep digging?" Claudia smiled slightly.

"I don't know. Want to go to the mall? They're having a sale on sweaters."

"No." Claudia stood up, suddenly decided. "I'm going to go see my lawyer."

"Your lawyer? Since when do you have a lawyer?"

"Since yesterday," Claudia replied. "She gave me her card. Glenda French."

16

For a moment, in front of Glenda's office, Claudia hesitated, her hand on the door. She still held that vision of Glenda and Mr. Xavier walking together—still felt that deep embarrassment at having imagined, even in her most secret fantasies, that he might have the slightest interest in her. Glenda was his lover. Of course. Glenda was exactly right for him.

She almost felt that Glenda knew her feelings, had traced them and smiled at them from the start. Suppose the two of them talked about it? The idea filled Claudia with horror. Still, determinedly, she went in.

In that instant the transition was made. Glenda, at her desk and steeped in books and papers, looked up, astonished, immediately delighted.

"Claudia! I'm so glad to see you." She leaped up, came around the desk. "I've been buried under paperwork all morning. Sit down! Sit down! Tell me what's new. Are you hungry?"

Without waiting for a reply Glenda disappeared into a small nook, returning with two dishes of rocky road ice cream.

"You don't need to be hungry for this." She grinned.

"How do you stay so thin?"

"I burn it off in here—that's for sure. Mmm." She took the ice cream eagerly, savoring it. "Delicious."

"My favorite flavor," Claudia said.

It was impossible not to love Glenda, to want to tell her everything, sitting here eating ice cream together as if they were old friends.

Claudia talked for nearly an hour, and Glenda listened, nodding, murmuring, understanding.

"So—that moment at the swim meet, something must have happened to me. I felt changed," Claudia said. "Everything I had read came together in that moment. It was strange."

Glenda watched Claudia, fascinated. "Your consciousness," she said at last, "had been raised."

Claudia inhaled deeply. "Is that it? What it's called?"

Glenda chuckled. "That's one definition. So now, what are you going to do?"

"What are my choices?"

Glenda pondered. "You can go along with Dr. Wallenburg. Or let her expel you."

"Let her expel me? Why would I?"

"Because that's something you can fight. Even if she only suspends you again, you could ask for a hearing. You would get your say."

"A hearing? Would other people be there?"

"Yes. People who are interested in this. Maybe even those biddies from that Women's League Committee." Her eyes were fixed on Claudia, challenging.

"Or," Glenda continued, "you can be a good girl. Promise not to cause any more trouble. Save your dad a lot of grief."

"He's furious at me!"

"I'll bet he is."

"Mr. Xavier says his job is on the line."

"Oh, really?"

"Dr. Wallenburg could fire him. He hasn't got tenure."

"But she'd need grounds. What would it be?" Glenda asked, eyes piercing. "Teaching you about your legal rights? Telling you this is supposed to be a free country? Is that what they'd fire him for?"

"I—they'd find some excuse."

"Of course they could. They always can. That's how they hold us in line."

They regarded each other silently, tensely.

"They always want to make you believe you don't have choices. But you do," Glenda said softly.

"I guess I knew that," Claudia said. "After I read those books. For the first time, I felt I didn't have to be . . ."

Glenda nodded. "Passive. You didn't have to be silent anymore. The earth wouldn't open up and swallow Claudia if she talked, even if she got mad and yelled, right?"

"Right." Claudia smiled.

"It's all very subtle," Glenda said. "And vicious. Don't rock the boat, honey, and you won't get hurt. Go hide in the office. Pick up other people's trash on Saturdays. Humiliate, degrade and disenfranchise yourself. Then we will let you go back to being a good, obedient little girl. Our nice little puppet. And, while you're picking up the trash—smile. Oh, yes. *Smile!*"

Glenda sat back, her cheeks flaming, her eyes deep and flickering.

"I hate to see them do it to you," she said at last, wearily. "You and I are—*simpatico.*"

Claudia knew the word.

"You understand?"

"I take Spanish."

"It's a special word, for certain friends. A person you feel close to right away. *Simpatico.*"

Claudia said, "I felt that way when you first came to our class."

"I want to tell you something." Glenda pushed herself away from the desk, turned so that Claudia saw only her profile, while Glenda looked out to the street.

"My real name is Glenda Fernandez. Does that mean anything to you?"

"Spanish," she said. Of course. Her high color—those dark, blazing eyes.

"Mexican. Chicana. I changed my name." Glenda paused, as if expecting a retort.

"Twelve years ago," she continued, "when I decided to go to law school, Mexican chiquitas were not considered very good potential as attorneys. When I told my counselor in school that I wanted to be a lawyer, you should have seen his face! The next week, in cooking class, we all made enchiladas. Guess who was asked to demonstrate? I wanted to throw the mess right in her face. Do you understand?"

"I think so."

"But how can I expect you to understand? There is so much I want to tell you. About why we have to fight. We are together in this. Sisters."

Claudia's gaze followed Glenda's—she felt a great surge of love. "What can we do?"

"You could call Dr. Wallenburg's bluff. At the same time have an opportunity to be heard."

"Mr. Xavier wants me to back off."

"Of course he does. That makes it nice and easy for everyone." She paused, faced Claudia squarely. "Look, Claudia. I know what you're thinking. Philip is a wonderful person—intelligent, really very liberal. But he's a man. And that makes him afraid."

"Of me?"

"Of losing. To a woman."

"But what can I possibly take away from him?"

"His superiority. His illusions."

"It's his job he's worried about," Claudia said.

"Of course. For a man, the job is always the same as the

self. That's why they fight us. They say they want us to have equal rights. But they refuse to move over where it counts, in the job market. That's where it's at."

"Yes." Claudia thought of her mother, sitting there drying her nails—it seemed ages ago.

"You see," Glenda persisted, "you don't have to be the scapegoat. You can challenge the principal. You don't have to hide during noontime or any of that. She's only trying to placate that Women's League. Apparently they've got a stranglehold on the board, and the board holds Dr. Wallenburg's job. So she's going to the weakest link—putting pressure on you."

"I'm the weakest link? Not very flattering."

"You're under her power. You're a student. She's already seen that your parents won't back you up."

"True." Claudia sighed deeply.

Glenda went to the bookshelf, brought down a volume. She pored over it for a time, then returned to her desk. "The education code states that students who are suspended from school have the right to a hearing by the superintendent. They can be confronted by their accusers. The principal can't expel you—she can only recommend it to the school board. If you have a hearing, you can have counsel."

"I'd like to see Mildew's face!"

"Who?"

"We call him Mildew. Mr. Milden, vice-principal."

Glenda laughed. "That's great; *Mildew*. What do they call Philip?"

Claudia sobered. "They call him the greatest teacher in the school," she said.

It hung between them. Glenda sighed deeply. "This would not hurt him, you know. In the long run, when women and men stand together, both are the winners."

"I've read that," said Claudia.

"It isn't just a question of wearing tops or not."

"Would they go into that at the hearing?"

"They'd have to. You challenged a sacred cow. The idea that women's breasts must be hidden. Why? Because they're obscene. Because they arouse men. Does that make any sense? Do you think for a moment that if women claimed men's hands turned them on, all men would wear gloves?"

Claudia shook her head. "I don't know."

"You don't have to decide anything now. Let it settle in your mind." She smiled self-consciously. "I've decided something. I'm going to change my name back again. I—I was a coward. I'll petition the court to change it back."

"I like Glenda Fernandez," Claudia said shyly.

"Listen, my friend. If you decide to have that hearing, I will represent you. If you want me to."

"Of course I'd want you!"

"I would be there with you. All the way."

"What about Mr.—Philip?"

Glenda laughed. She did not respond, except with a gesture.

17

After I left Glenda, I spent hours just walking. I went past the old farms and small stores by the railroad track; I didn't want to go home. It was as if I had a premonition.

I only wanted to escape. Part of me longed to fight, to be Glenda's partner in a noble undertaking. But the idea of going to a hearing, facing all those people, hostile and condemning, filled me with dread. Worse, I wondered about my own judgment. What if they were right? What if my little cause opened up a whole Pandora's box of troubles, allowed those raucous and restless kids free reign—those kids who were always in trouble?

My mind flashed back to an occurrence of a few months ago. I had been driving with Vivian. Suddenly the traffic stopped; red lights flashed, and then we saw the tangle of twisted steel and glass, two figures laid prone on the freeway. We saw splotches of blood in the road. Later that night on the evening news it turned out one man had been driving while drunk, in fact, had been involved in sixteen accidents in the past two years. "The law is too permissive," they quoted the DA. "The courts have been too concerned with rights and no balance of responsibility."

I walked on, cutting across a field of green wild wheat. I knew Glenda expected great things of me. What if I couldn't deliver? I wished I could just lie down there in the field and sleep, sleep for a year.

At home I knew immediately that something was wrong. My mother sat in the living room, her hands idle in her lap. No music. No mending or reading or cutting out recipes; she simply sat there with the curtains drawn. My father was not yet home.

"What's wrong?"

"Oh, Claudia," she moaned.

I pulled open the curtains. "Mom! What's happened?"

"I got a call from Mrs. Athay."

"Your boss!"

"My district manager for LovLee. She's never phoned me before, except when I won the prize. She phoned me then. To congratulate me."

My mother was not crying, except inside. Tiredness showed in her voice, an inability to fight anymore. I knew the feeling.

"So, what did she say?"

"She told me that my—my involvement in what's been happening—giving a statement to the newspaper, and you doing—what you've been doing—what you did. . . . She said it gives LovLee Cosmetics a bad image. She said they've been trying to build an image of wholesomeness." She lifted her hands to her temples, let them drop down into her lap.

"Are they saying you can't have a personal life?" I exclaimed. "How can they dictate to you?"

"Claudia. They can choose who should represent them. Mrs. Athay said they have to be very particular. She said it had nothing to do with me personally, but that these things hit some people the wrong way. And LovLee has spent hundreds of thousands of dollars building its reputation."

"What did you tell her?" I demanded. "Did you tell her to take her stupid job and—"

"Don't yell, Claudia." Mom sighed. "I can't take it now."

I went and fixed dinner. Broiled chicked and salad. I took a "bake and serve" bread from the freezer and put it in the oven, dished out two kinds of jam—my mother loves fresh hot bread.

When my dad came in, he knew immediately that something was wrong. I heard them talking in the living room. For a while my father just listened. Then he said, "All right, Doreen. I tell you, that job wasn't good enough for you anyway. To tell you the truth, I wasn't thrilled about having you go into other people's houses selling things. Who needs it? I make a good living. I always thought this cosmetic thing was—well—beneath you."

Silence. And then, "I loved it."

"Well. It isn't the worst thing in the world, Doreen. Maybe you'll find another job. Something with a little more class."

They came in to eat. I excused myself. I couldn't stand it. In my room I turned on the stereo to drown out their talk.

I heard a tapping at my window. For some reason the only person I could think of was David Beckett. Would he come here? Might he try to sweet talk me now? How dare he!

I was furious, my heart pounding with indignation.

With the next tapping came a voice. "Claudia! Let me in."

It was Bennie. She looked like a phantom, wearing a dark sweater and jeans. She thrust one sneaker up onto the windowsill, hoisted herself over, looking around like a criminal avoiding the cops.

I couldn't help laughing. "Bennie! What are you doing?"

She pulled herself inside, and I saw she was shivering. She looked worried and tired. "I had to see you," she whispered. "I didn't want to ring the bell and disturb your folks."

"It's after midnight!" I exclaimed, keeping my voice down.

"I waited until my folks were asleep. I snuck out."

"Oh, Bennie." I hugged her.

She stood there twisting her hands, and she said, "Now I don't even know what to say to you. I've thought about everything for hours and hours. I even read some of those books you told me about."

Briefly I told her about Dr. Wallenburg's ultimatum—my choices. "I have a chance now to make a real contribution," I said. "I can fight this. I can really test the law."

Bennie smiled slightly. "Like Joan of Arc. You can lead the battle."

"Yes. If you want to be dramatic about it."

"It is dramatic," said Bennie. "Like a protest march or a revolution. Like those women I read about who chained themselves to the city hall to get the vote."

"It's not like that," I argued. "Getting a hearing is the legal way to change things."

"Like going to court?"

"Not exactly. A hearing is similar, though. It would be open to the public."

The thought of it made Bennie flush. "I'd die," she said. "Simply die."

"No, you wouldn't," I said. "Look, you came here. You didn't die."

"But I was petrified!" Suddenly she laughed. "I'll admit it was sort of exciting." Then she grew sober. "I don't know what's right," she said. "I'm sure women have been treated unfairly . . ."

"Oppressed," I said.

"All right." She waved me aside. "Even so. Some of them are going too far. They don't like the way the world is, so they blame men for everything. That isn't fair either."

"But I'm talking about the law. Illegal discrimination. Standing up for your rights."

"I read about that, too. And I sort of understand what you were doing at that swim meet. Still, I know I'd never do it. I'm too modest. Call it uptight if you want. And"—she looked at me straight on without flinching—"I don't think it really proved anything, Claudia. But . . ." She smiled. "I still love you. I want us always to be friends."

We embraced. "Me too," I said.

Then I helped her out the window and watched her run across the yard, looking like a dark shadow, and I marveled that she had come.

Sometime later in the night I woke up. I must have had a dream. I don't know what it was. But I woke up with a sense of certainty. Suddenly it didn't matter what might happen to me. I saw myself as part of a long, long parade. I could stop and turn back, betray all the other marchers. Or I could move ahead.

Two main words rang in my head. Power. Pressure. Two terrible words, always applied by the strong against the weak.

I thought of poor Mom, done out of her job.

I thought of Bennie, having to sneak out at night like a bandit, but doing it to tell me she loved me.

I thought of how complex it all was; I never wanted a riot or even a cause. But there it was, like a package someone had dropped at my feet. I could either pick it up and run with it, or let it lie, maybe to be lost forever.

The next morning I went straight to Dr. Wallenburg's office. I told her my decision. I kept it simple; I'm not good with speeches.

I said, "Dr. Wallenburg, I'm going to request a hearing by the superintendent."

She stared at me in shocked silence. "A hearing?"

"I know I am entitled under the Education Code to have a hearing about my suspension. And I know you will suspend

130

me, because I am not going to be able to—to comply with your demands."

Her face became very red, then dangerously pale. "Who told you these words? Who has tutored you for this?"

"Nobody. I'm doing it because—because it is my right."

"You realize," Dr. Wallenburg said, "that if your suspension is upheld, the school board will certainly vote to expel you."

"I realize that."

Dr. Wallenburg heaved back in her chair. All the breath seemed to have gone out of her. At last she nodded. "I hope you know what you're doing, Claudia."

I went to my locker and gathered up my things. It would be at least two weeks before a hearing could be arranged. Meanwhile, I'd study at home.

Furry happened to walk by my locker. I told him my decision.

He drove me home. At my door he gave me a quick kiss. "You're quite a gal!" he said.

Then I went to bed and slept for the next six hours.

18

Many weeks ago my dad had taken my watch in to be fixed. He'd given it to me for my sixteenth birthday. He had snapped my picture as I opened the box and grinned, calling, "Time marches on!"

Tuesday night, home from work, he laid the watch on the little hall table. "I brought your watch back," he said, our first direct conversation in days.

"Thank you, Dad."

Usually he'd have said how much it cost to fix. He always did that.

"How much was it?"

"A few bucks. I don't remember exactly."

I glanced up at him. When had his shoulders begun to stoop? Once, he was the strongest man in the world, holding me safe at the deep end of the swimming pool, pulling me back from a huge truck in the street.

"It looks like new," I said.

"Well, they cleaned it."

He stood awkwardly by, watching me fasten the watch on my wrist. Then he said, "I saw this thing today in the watch store, a printed saying on the wall. Something about I do my thing and you do yours, and I'm not in this world to live up to your expectations. You know what I mean? Have you seen something like it?"

"I think so. Maybe."

"Well, I don't agree with it." He paused, seemed to be struggling to collect the right words. "See, I don't think everybody can just go around doing their own thing. What if they did? What would the world be like?"

I said nothing, wondering what he might consider as doing "his own thing" all the time—probably fishing.

"Of course, times are changing. And it's not all bad. Some of the new ways are—well, they're good. But a person can't change all at once. You know what I mean?"

"I think so."

He looked at me and seemed about to say more, then turned and stormed out to the kitchen calling, "Doreen! When are we going to eat, for God's sake?"

After dinner they stayed in the kitchen. They drank tea, which my mother brewed in a blue and white pot covered with an old-fashioned tea cozy.

We'd had it for years. It was obviously handmade. Strange, how now it suddenly aroused my interest. "Where did we get this?" I fingered the bright yarn.

"I knitted it," Mom said.

"When?"

"Oh, I suppose I was just about your age. No, a little younger. Fifteen, I guess."

Somehow, it made me sad. "May I be excused?"

"Fine. If you want to do the dishes in the morning."

But in my room I could not concentrate on anything.

I decided to go to the kitchen and do up the dishes. Out in the hall I heard them. How could it be that all these years they never knew that we listened from the hall?

". . . why Mrs. Norford called you that day. She was trying to be subtle. You just didn't pick it up."

"How could I possibly have known that? How do *you* know?"

"Because Bud Norford called me this afternoon."

I pressed myself against the wall. From here I could see their shadows against the kitchen wall. It almost seemed as if I were a puppeteer and they the puppets, and that by willing it I could make them move and speak and cast that silhouette on the white kitchen wall.

". . . he made me an offer."

"An offer, Walt?"

"He just about out and told me, Doreen, that if I can get Claudia not to press things at that hearing—get her to apologize and lie low—he'd see to it that I get all the district's insurance contracts. You see, the board's divided into two factions. Those behind Spengler want to make this a big deal—show how terrible the schools are, kids going wild and everything, so they can get a different guy elected up in Sacramento."

"Why should Claudia care about that?"

"Those on Norford's side want this all to blow over quietly. It's political," he explained.

"You'd get all those insurance contracts?"

"All. You know what that would mean. Norford isn't only on the school board. He has connections all over town."

"What did you tell him, Walt?"

"What did I tell him? What do you think I told him, Doreen? I told him my daughter is not for sale, that's what I told him! I told him I don't buy and sell her as if she was a piece of meat, for God's sake!"

His voice dropped, barely audible. "I don't like what she did. I hate it. But, my God, she's a *person*."

19

The reporter, Stan Bliss, talked to each of us separately. He became the go-between when the TV station people came out to do some preliminary work for their documentary, "Schools in Transition."

But that came much later. You probably saw it. Complete with me standing at the hearing and telling them . . .

But, I'm getting ahead of my story.

Stan Bliss came out to my house. We sat together on the old hammock out back, and I was amazed how three hours passed so quickly. He was terrific. We laughed a lot. He listens and asks questions and really concentrates on what you're saying. He doesn't judge. He doesn't twist things or plan how he'll get you to reveal yourself; he's really honest.

It turned out he really did know Scott. Stan was a little older, but he and Scott used to play basketball together in high school. Stan graduated from college in three years—Durant College. They let you go at your own pace.

He told me, "I don't make my living distorting people's lives. I don't like being manipulated. And I don't do it to other people either."

I understood that. I admired it. Still, I teased him. "Of

course, some reporters will hang around forever at a high school, just waiting to catch some girl . . ." I blushed. ". . . rebelling."

He laughed and took my hand. "I was lucky," he said. He squeezed my hand. "I mean it." He became serious. "From now on," he said, "it's going to be rough."

"I know."

"Unfortunately, some of the media people will try to make that hearing into a circus."

He held my hand very tightly, and then he put his arms around me, nothing more, but I felt a thrill in his nearness that I had never known before except in fantasy.

"You know," Stan said, "if you hadn't asked for this suspension hearing, I think Milden or Mr. Spengler would have engineered it."

"I don't understand."

Stan put his finger on my brow, gently stroking me. "Don't frown. I'll explain. They need a cause to rally around. Spengler needs an issue."

"Why? He's already president of the school board."

"He wants to run for the state legislature. That's big time. The road to Washington, D.C."

"So he's got to go on a big crusade," I said. "Clean up the mess in our schools. That makes him the perfect candidate."

"It also gets him the support of the Women's League Committee."

"But what about Dr. Wallenburg? All along, I had the strange feeling that in a way she almost agreed with me. That she might even have taken my side, if only . . ."

"She's been pressured plenty by Mr. Spengler. You're pretty perceptive, you know?" He kissed me lightly on the chin. "I think she does sympathize with you. But her job's at stake. Spengler probably threatened to have her fired if she didn't come down hard on you. He could do it, too. She doesn't have tenure in this district."

"What makes you think she's sympathetic?"

Stan brought out his small notebook, flipped it open. "A little research." He smiled proudly. "It seems that Muriel Wallenburg was quite a pistol in her youth. She went to U.C. Berkeley in the sixties. She was in on some of those sit-ins. There's even a record of her arrest—something about taking over the showroom of an automobile dealer."

"At least we know she was a kid once," I said grinning. "I'm not so sure about Mildew. I think he was born with that sour look on his face."

Stan shook his head, saying, "I think he really cares about education. He's a little old-fashioned."

"That's putting it mildly!"

"I figure, if Spengler wins the nomination for state legislature, he'll have to quit the school board. That would leave an opening. My guess is that Cave Milden would love to be on the school board—and we know who would support him."

"But he'd have to quit as vice principal."

"Sure. I think he'd like a good excuse to quit. The man's worn out. I feel sorry for him."

I looked up at Stan. I'd never known anyone so fair, so sweet, so completely warm and—and human. The next moment his arms came around me. He kissed me. "You," he whispered, close to my lips, "are very special."

He kissed me again, and I felt a yearning. He was completely different from any boy or man I'd ever known. I felt completely safe in his arms.

I took a deep breath. "I have lots to do," I said. "And some decisions to make."

He smiled, nodding. "I know."

"Any advice?"

He held me away, shaking his head. "Oh, no, you don't. I wouldn't dare presume to offer you advice. This is one lady who makes her own decisions."

My decision to go through with the hearing had sent

Glenda into immediate action. She was thrilled. It involved an enormous amount of preparation. I spent some time at her office every day. We talked. I read while she pored through the law books. We must have eaten gallons of rocky road ice cream.

It was terrifically exciting being with Glenda. She was all fire and elation.

"I knew you'd do it! I knew right away you weren't afraid to put yourself on the line. We're going to fight this—oh, man, are we going to fight. They'll be sorry they took us on. We'll show them what freedom really means."

I had decided not to drag my parents into this. Glenda told me I needed an adult to file the request for a hearing.

"I'm not even asking my parents," I said. "I want you to do it for me. Is that all right?"

"Sure. I can sign as your *guardian ad litem*. Just for this particular hearing. And for any further litigation that results from it."

"Further litigation? What do you mean? I thought the superintendent will decide at the hearing whether the suspension was justified or not."

"That's true. Basically, the hearing will concern your initial act—taking off your top at the swim meet. What we're going to do is show that the school rule allowing boys to go naked on top, but not girls, is discriminatory. Because it makes judgements about the female body that have nothing to do with their rights as *people*. The female breast is not a sex object—except as men make it so. It is not involved in reproduction. Women without breasts can have babies. Fifty years ago, men who exposed their chests on the beach were arrested. That shows you, it's just the attitude we have to fight."

"Because *any* discrimination"—I nodded—"leads to inequality."

"Correct."

"But what will the school do? Would they have to say

they were wrong, and that girls *can* go topless? Is this what we're fighting for? If so, I don't want to—"

"That's not your problem!" Glenda cried. "You don't have to worry about all the repercussions. Maybe they'll make a rule saying that *no* students, neither boys nor girls, can go topless at school. That's fine. At least it's equal."

I wasn't sure how I felt about that. I talked it over with Stan Bliss. "If every person pushes and stretches the law for his own point, what happens?"

"You get a heck of a lot of new laws and restrictions," he said.

"Some people lose freedom that way. The boys at school would lose the freedom to go topless."

"True. It's complicated." He smiled and gave me a peppermint. That's what he always does when the talk gets deep. He reaches into that huge pocket in his raincoat and pulls out a peppermint for me.

I hadn't figured on getting to like him so much. And the other thing I hadn't figured on was my mother's reaction when I told her Glenda was signing the suspension hearing request.

My mother's face changed so that I thought she would scream. But she only stared at me, her eyes turning black with anger, and then she cried, "How could you do this to me?"

"What? What have I done? I was only trying to save you the problem."

"How could you?" she gasped. "You didn't even ask me. Your own mother. Maybe I wanted to be involved. Did you ever think of that? Maybe I had something to offer. But you asked this stranger."

"Mom—I wanted to make it easy for you," I cried. "I didn't want you and Dad to get into a fight over it."

"Maybe I didn't want it to be easy!" she exclaimed. "Why didn't you think of me? Just me?"

Later that night I heard them again. My mother's voice

was very low, her words infrequent. It was my father who did most of the talking.

He was in a good mood. He had come to some kind of peace with himself about the hearing, I guess. He wasn't planning to attend, but he had stopped giving me those awful looks and he was talking to me.

His voice was eager. ". . . it would be good for both of us, Doreen. After all, you've learned something about business now, and I can really use an extra pair of hands in the office. You could answer my phone. You could sit at a desk in the hall, be a receptionist. You have nice clothes."

"But what would I actually *do*, Walt?"

"You'd be my assistant, that's what you'd do!"

"You mean I'd have to learn about insurance?"

"No, no. I wouldn't expect you to bother with that. No. You'd answer the phone, like I said, and maybe take a letter once in a while, do some filing. I'd teach you how to file. Go out for things—you know, maybe do the banking. Make coffee."

"I don't know, Walt. I'm used to keeping my own schedule."

"It would be fun, Doreen. You would enjoy it. We would be partners."

"Would I get paid?"

In the silence I imagined his face puffing up, halfway between laughter and rage. "You want to be *paid?*"

"I like to have a little pin money."

He laughed. "You are really something. Well, well. So we take money out of one pocket and put it into the other. You want to be paid for working at *our own place?* Well, let's start you out for a month, see how you do. Then, maybe we can work something out. Is that what you want? Your own bank account? Pin money?"

I heard nothing more. Inside, I ached.

Maybe it was this that finally got to me. Maybe I just got sick and tired of standing in the hall listening, having my emotions pushed and pulled into awkward shapes until I no longer knew who I was or whom I was fighting for.

Still, it wasn't until the last day before the hearing that it all came together for me. From Scott, a phone call.

"Hang in there, babe!" He sounded exuberant, free. He had his plans all set for next semester in Madrid. "Look, I'm going to work all summer. If you work too, maybe between us we can save enough to have you come visit me the following summer in Spain. How about it?"

I loved the idea. I loved Scott. I told him so. For the first time since babyhood I said the words, "I love you, Scott!"

"And I love you." He tried to make it light. "Hang in there!"

Later Glenda came by. She looked tired and thinner than ever, but her eyes glowed with a brightness I could now understand, for I had felt it, too. Her movements were quick, almost erratic. She opened her notebook, sat down at the dining room table, spreading out her things, pointing to passages she had marked.

She talked to me about tomorrow. What I must say. How I should look.

She handed me a white box tied with a bright gold ribbon.

"What's this?" I was truly surprised. "I should be the one buying you a present."

She smiled. "I thought you might like something new to wear at the hearing."

I opened the box. Inside, folded in white tissue paper, was a white blouse with a high neck, a little ruffle at the edge with prim little white buttons. The long sleves were edged with the same ruffle.

I held it out. It was the right size. But I had never in my life worn anything like it.

Glenda laughed. "Look, I know it isn't anything smashing. But you're not supposed to look sexy at this hearing. We want you looking very young and girlish and demure."

"This blouse will certainly do it," I said faintly.

"Wear a plain skirt, nothing bright or too short. Do you have something plain?"

"Yes."

"Terrific. What about shoes? You can't wear sandals or—"

"I have shoes," I told her.

She sat back. She seemed suddenly spent, even half dreaming, her eyes distant and her breathing deep. Somehow, she seemed removed from me and this room, from everything except an idea that held her attention completely as she talked and talked.

". . . never know where a thing like this will lead. How far it will go. A case a few years ago ended up in the state supreme court. A test case . . . making new law . . . can you imagine the feeling? For years, forever, people read about it and quote it . . . all my life I've wanted to be where the action is, where it really is."

"Glenda." I stopped her. "What are you saying? That you're not just working on tomorrow's hearing? That you want me to go to court about this?"

She pulled out of her dream, eyed me fiercely. "Why of course! What did you think? That I'd do all this work for one crummy hearing, a one-hour deal? Claudia, the best thing that can happen tomorrow is that the school board expels you! Imagine the publicity. Why do you think I've been working with this Bliss character, getting him to line up the TV people, getting all this ammunition? If we play it exactly right, you'll be a national figure. You'll be the plaintiff in a case that would take us all the way to the Supreme Court of the United States!"

"Glenda, I thought you wanted me to win."

"Of course I want you to win. But what is winning? Winning is not making one little point in one small battle. Winning means taking the whole show, don't you understand? We have a chance to make a landmark case here.

142

Have you any idea what that means? We'll be making *new law.*"

"But I'm not a lawyer—" I began.

"Look, the whole South was desegregated because one person fought the issue of separate drinking fountains. A small thing like that, but it paved the way for everything that followed."

"But they had a real issue!" I exclaimed. "It really isn't fair not to let people drink from a fountain. You told us this very thing in class. You said it was so bad that sometimes black people traveling in the south couldn't get any water or find any restrooms and had to use the fields . . ."

"Are you looking for the perfect cause?" she demanded. "Sorry, we aren't lucky enough to get the perfect cause on a silver platter. We have to make do with what we've got. Maybe your topless dispute isn't the best way to fight for equality, but it's all we've got right now. You've got to fight where you can. You've got to go all the way!"

It was then my parents came home. They had gone to an early movie. Some spy thing.

Hastily Glenda picked up her things and left.

Her words rang in my ears the whole night long.

I dreamed that weird dream again—the black woman with pendulous breasts, holding out the baby. "Don't you want this child? You birthed it. Don't you want this little baby? It's yours."

And when I looked amid the folds of the blanket and saw the creature wrapped inside, I was filled with such terror and revulsion at the monster that I awakened screaming. Actually, I had not uttered more than a groan. My room was silent. Down the hall, I knew, my parents slept soundly.

I lay there planning what I must do. My head was clear. I was absolutely sure.

20

I want to tell you about the hearing, because it was so frightening. Not that I feared what might happen to me, or how I'd be able to stand up in front of all those strangers and talk. No—what was frightening was the process itself, how it swallowed everyone up. It changed us all.

The room was set up to specifications; everyone in his place and orderly, with expressions fixed and ready, identical in the bland look they assumed.

I sat beside and a little behind the main table, so that everyone saw me, yet I was placed apart. My role was to be seen, to be judged, to be silent.

As the hearing progressed, I had the terrible sense that everyone here existed only to move this hearing along, that apart from this process we were nothing. People spoke, but only in crisp symbols. Everything was timed, like a movie reel unraveling, final and fixed.

Once there was twittering laughter over some silly thing. Even this seemed a fraud and purposely planned to try to deny the severity of what we were doing.

Strange, how procedures make robots out of people. I

felt reluctant to move or smile or even think any thoughts that would remove me from this place.

I listened as the superintendent made his opening announcement, introduced speakers by formal name and title. Nothing, nothing could break through the cold and calculated process that seemed to have assumed flesh and blood while we—all of us—were only its servants.

It began at nine-thirty in the morning. By nine the room was filled, and people were standing in the hall. When Glenda saw me, she stiffened.

"Why didn't you wear the blouse?" She seemed incredulous.

"I'm sorry, Glenda."

At that moment someone came up to her with a minicam, and it was the last thing I said to her.

Mr. Xavier was there, looking scholarly in gray slacks and tweed coat. As the hearing began, his face was set into a passive look, like one who has a distant but kindly interest in the proceedings.

Miss Merriman was there. Just before the hearing, out in the hall, she came to me. "Good luck, Claudia," she said, and she pressed my hand.

I took a deep breath. I wanted to speak with her, but then the gavel fell, the call for silence. The hearing began.

I won't bore you with all the details, with the opening speech by the superintendent and the impassioned stance of Rolf Spengler using all those emotional words detailing the "pathetic corruption of our youth," and the "malicious minds and ignorant do-gooders . . ."

I won't go into the somber and tedious repetition of the situation and charges, the detail upon detail of actions and reactions—I'll only mention, as I will remember forever, seeing my parents enter the hearing room several minutes after it had begun, seeing them sit down quietly to listen.

For the first time in my life I understood what it means to be grown.

As I sat up at the front listening, I felt torn in two, one of me watching, the other floating away into the future, unable to concentrate on the meaning of what was happening. When my name was called, I was startled.

"Claudia Gayle Warner!"

Glenda had prepared me. I was supposed to say only two words: they would ask, "Are you the petitioner in this hearing?" I would go to the microphone and respond, "Yes, sir."

"Claudia Gayle Warner!"

I went up to the microphone. In my hand I held a small card. On it I had written my ideas as they came to me in the middle of the night. Now the words came even more readily than they had when I first thought of them.

"Mr. Superintendent," I said, hearing the odd ringing quality of my voice echoing back at me through the microphone, "I have decided not to ask for a suspension hearing."

Silence gaped. Then pandemonium began.

The superintendent let his gavel fall. "What is the meaning of this, Miss Warner? I have your petition here! You have asked for a hearing. You have involved all these people, brought an attorney—"

"Yes, sir," I broke in, my voice ringing back again, "I did ask for a hearing. But that was before I realized what was happening. This hearing has nothing to do with me, or with what I did. It isn't even concerned with equal rights. Everybody here is—is doing his own thing. Doing it for his own reasons . . ."

"Miss Warner, we are not asking for your judgment!" cried Rolf Spengler, leaping to his feet, and again the gavel came down, and Glenda, unaccountably, stood up and cried, "I object!"

"Continue," said the superintendent gravely.

146

"I apologize for putting you and the board to this trouble," I said. My legs were still trembling, but somehow I felt lighter now, exuberantly so. "But I am withdrawing from this hearing. I am no longer a student at Menominee High. This morning I sent a letter to my high school and to the district office. I've withdrawn from school. I will get my diploma by taking the high school equivalency exam next month. Since I am no longer a student at Menominee High, I cannot be suspended or expelled."

The superintendent was astounded. "You mean you are walking away from this hearing?"

"Yes, I am, sir."

You can't imagine the outburst. Amid the uproar, a microphone was thrust before my face. "When did you become disillusioned with the hearing procedure?"

"Does this have anything to do with Mr. Spengler's candidacy for the legislature?"

"Who advised you to do this?"

"Have you been working with the ACLU?"

"What are your plans for the future?"

I began to laugh. They must have thought I'd gone crazy. While the reporters with their microphones stumbled all over each other trying to get me to respond, Stan came rushing to take my arm and pull me away, calling disgustedly, "Nobody had to advise her! The lady has a mind of her own!"

We had a few moments together outside on the street, before the cameramen and reporters caught up again.

"I don't want you to think I'm just afraid," I gasped.

"No way. It takes courage to defy both sides—to really think for yourself. Now they're all going to be screaming at you." He held my arm very tightly, and I leaned close to him for a moment.

"In a way, I really did want to fight," I told him. "I wanted to be in the center of it—have a cause. You know?"

He nodded. "Of course."

"But to fight just for the sake of fighting . . ." I shook my head. The reporters were coming. I had so little time! ". . . means you never really win anything. You just go through the motions. Stan, I don't want to be used."

The cameraman nearly tripped on his electrical cord in his haste to approach.

"Miss Warner! Some people are saying you planned this all along, that you only wanted the publicity."

"No comment," I said.

"Did you consult with your attorney about leaving this hearing?"

"No. My attorney knew nothing about it. I—I'm afraid I left her in the lurch."

"Why have you chosen to abandon this cause, Miss Warner?"

I looked at the man, at the camera. There was so much I would have wanted to say about winning or losing, fighting or waiting to fight another day. I wanted to talk about finding the right time and the right cause, being ready for it, seizing the moment not because other people stand to gain extra advantages, but because it's really important.

But I'm not good at making speeches.

A woman reporter ran up and called out, "Don't you believe in freedom, Miss Warner? What about women's rights?"

"I do believe in freedom," I told her. "That's the whole point."

One thing more. About four weeks after the hearing, I received a letter from Durant College.

Dear Applicant:

Due to a recent expansion of our program, we find that several positions in the freshman class at Durant College have become available.

We have reviewed your application and are happy to offer you enrollment at Durant College for the fall semester.

Durant College seeks students of independent spirit and critical attitude, who will preserve and enhance our democratic traditions.

We sincerely hope that your experience at Durant College will be rewarding.

About the Author

SONIA LEVITIN has written numerous prize-winning books for young people, covering a broad range of subjects—from picture books to historical, contemporary and humorous novels. She also writes for adults under another name.

She was born in Germany and escaped to the United States during the Hitler period—which accounts in part for her great concern for freedom, a theme in many of her books, covering the range from political to personal and spiritual freedom.

Her interests include history, music, travel and, of course, reading. She has been a teacher for most of her adult life—usually teaching courses in creative writing, but she has also taught English, citizenship and American history.

She lives with her husband, two German shepherds and a cat in southern California, spending holidays with their two grown children, Daniel and Shari.